Published 1981 by
The Hamlyn Publishing Group Limited
London · New York · Sydney · Toronto
Astronaut House, Feltham, Middlesex, England
© Copyright The Hamlyn Publishing Group Limited 1981

ISBN 0 600 33745 6

Printed in Italy

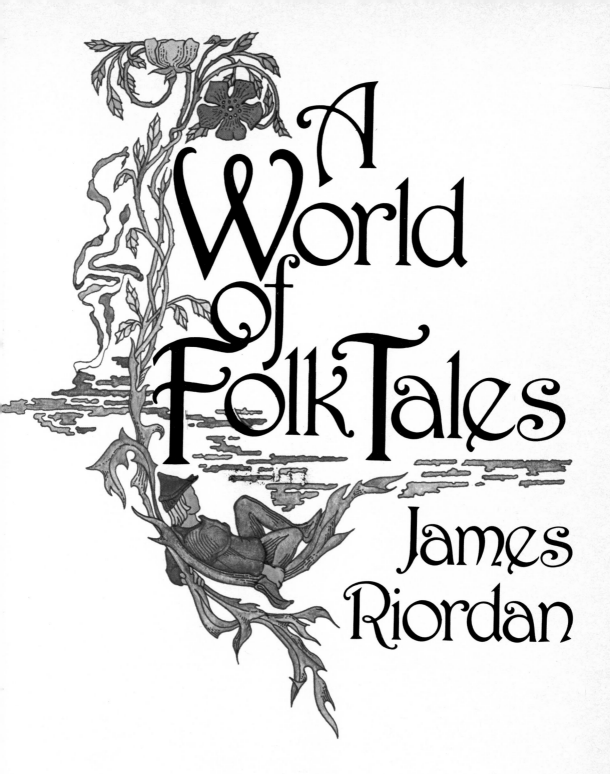

A World of Folk Tales

James Riordan

Hamlyn

London · New York · Sydney · Toronto

Contents

Introduction

I once met a man up in the Arctic who told me what folk tales meant to him. There we were, some half dozen grown men, sitting in the half dark of a walrus tent, washing down whale meat with a potent green brew, swapping folk yarns. This man, a wizened old Eskimo, was saying that when he was a lad no one for hundreds of miles around could read or write; there were no nurseries or schools, no radio or television, no newspapers or books, no churches or bibles. But there were folk tales. When the children came home to their tents from a hard day on the ice, they enjoyed the happiest times of their short lives: the treasured hour of storytelling.

'Grannie or Grandad would sit closer to the fire, pull a rabbit skin rug round them and begin a story,' the old Eskimo told me. 'The stories taught us to understand and love the beauty of life, to be brave and to fight evil. And now, when I recall my cold and hungry childhood, I wonder what life would have been like for little children if it had not been for those wonderful stories.'

I've never forgotten those words. They opened my eyes to the importance of folk tales in the lives of everyone not so long ago. How lucky we are to have enough to eat, to be warm or cool as the fancy takes us, to have plenty of leisure time and a choice of many activities to fill it, and how lucky we are to be able to read in our own tongue tales from all over the world.

Some people may be tempted to look for a meaning in these tales. But perhaps we should not try to be too wise. One lesson that my twenty years' wandering in folk tale realms has taught me, is that the tales have many, many meanings. The one feeling that does seem common to all folk tales is that of *Hope*. The Russian writer Maxim Gorky put it thus: 'In folk tales people fly through the air on a magic carpet, walk in seven-league boots, build castles overnight. Tales opened up for me a new world where some free and fearless power reigned and inspired in me a dream of a better life.'

When people have to struggle against the elements to survive or when they remain poor despite their hard work and honesty, then they may dream of inheriting the earth by magical means. And what ogre would deny them that?

The tales I have presented here are all bound by Hope; and by Hope's dream of a better life filled with love and beauty, peace and togetherness.

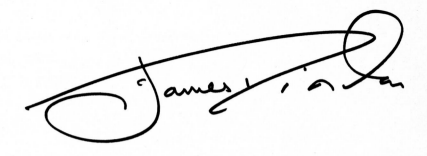

Kwaku Ananse and the Python

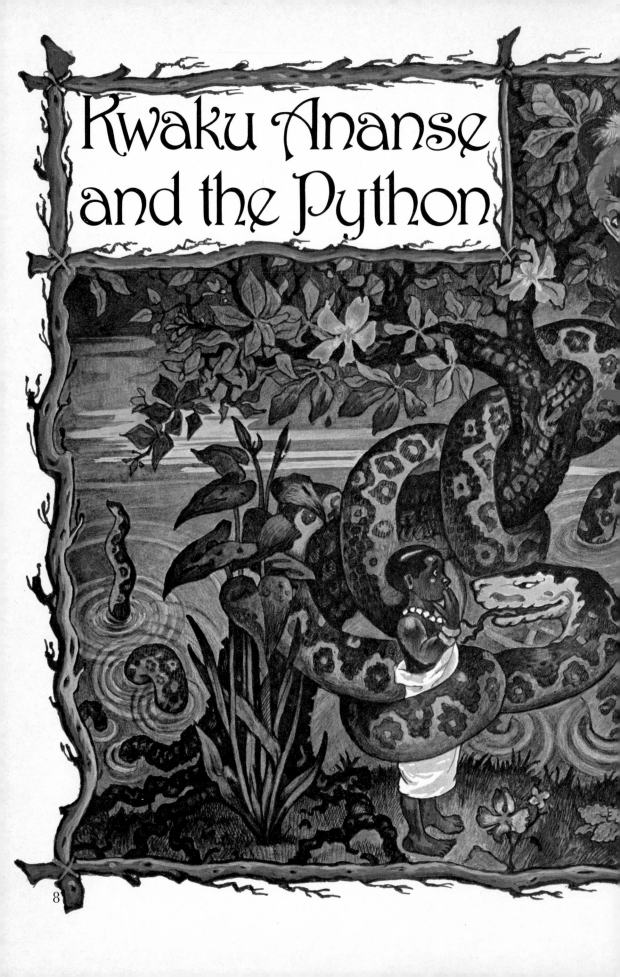

Listen, now, my children, to how that cunning old rascal Kwaku Ananse the Spider Man caught the greedy python.

Once there was a village in Ashanti lands upon the banks of the Niger River in Africa. Alas, alas, a black cloud of gloom hung above that village. For a giant python dwelt within the river bank and ate all who came near the water. Sometimes he would drop from a tree upon a little child, and coil his fat sides around it, and swallow it whole, in a single gulp. Or he would take a goat or sheep, or even a cow, as it came down to the river to drink.

The people grieved, grieved, grieved. They did not know what to do. Finally, an assembly of all the elders was called and it was decided to send a messenger to Nyame the Sky God. Surely, they thought, he would take pity on them and rid them of the evil snake.

When the great Sky God heard their complaint, he scratched his head and fell to thinking.

'Tch, tch, tch,' he said at last perplexed. 'You see, my children, that python is my child too. Though I much regret his disgraceful manners, I cannot judge between you. But there is in the next village a man called Kwaku Ananse, who thinks that he is very clever. I am sick and tired of his boastfulness. So go to this man and tell him this: if he rids you of the python, then I shall believe he is indeed extremely wise, and I shall reward him richly with even more wisdom. If he fails, he shall be punished.'

The messenger bore the Sky God's words back to the Ashanti village, then went off to find Kwaku Ananse the Spider Man. He found the skinny old man at home, having a meal with his wife Aso in their hut. When Kwaku Ananse heard that the Sky God had cast a shadow on his wisdom, he chuckled loudly.

'Oho, hee, hee, hee. Everybody knows how wise I am,' he said. 'I shall help you with your problem, sure enough. Now, how big is this python? Is he longer than my hut?'

'Much, much longer, longer,' the messenger replied.

'Is he longer than the Chief's hut?' asked Kwaku Ananse.

'Much, much longer, longer,' came the reply.

'Is he as long as six huts together?'

'That's about the length,' the man said, 'but he is also

very fat and strong.'

Kwaku Ananse smiled a broad, broad smile.

'Listen well,' he said. 'Tomorrow morning at first dawn, your men must bring to the river bank a big, big bowl of powdered yam, some eggs and a calabash of good palm wine, and I will deal with this wicked snake. But should that fat serpent get the better of old Kwaku, you must promise me a splendid funeral. Your girls must shave their heads and you must bury me in a fine kente cloth with kuduo pots at my head and a gold ring on my finger.'

The deal was struck.

Next morning at first light, Kwaku took his axe and went into the jungle. He chopped down a straight young tree and several twining creepers to make strong ropes. Then, calling his several children to help him, he carried the log down to the river. Already, the big bowl of powdered yam, eggs and a calabash of palm wine were waiting for him beneath a palm tree. The villagers had left the bowls and run back home before the python could swallow them up.

In the distance Kwaku Ananse could hear the beat, beat, beating of the funeral drums. He smiled to himself; so sure were the villagers that the python would kill him, they were already playing his funeral song.

Anyone who had remained to watch Kwaku Ananse would have been puzzled by his actions. First he sat himself down on a tree stump upon the river bank above the python's hole. Then he began a conversation with himself. One voice was high, high, high, and flattering; the other was low, low, low, and scornful. The python was woken up by these strange noises, and lay in his hole listening to the voices quarrelling.

'I tell you, I tell you,' said the high voice, 'he is so huge and fat and very, very beautiful. I cannot understand why the villagers dislike him. He is a very fine fellow, I tell you.'

'You lie, you lie,' came the deep voice, 'he is short and skinny, and very, very ugly. No wonder people hate him when he steals their beasts and children.'

'No, no, no, I tell you,' said the first voice again, 'the python is my friend. He's a very fine fellow indeed. It is not his fault that he gets hungry. If those mean Ashanti were to offer him some powdered yam, some eggs and a

calabash of good palm wine, he would not have to steal.'

'Who says Ashantis are mean! Who says Ashantis are mean!' growled the deep voice enraged. 'I'll make you eat your words.'

With that the python heard the thud, thud, thud of blows, and then he heard running feet. The deep voice was heard no more. Being very curious, he poked his head out of his hole to see who had spoken so highly of him. It was nothing but the truth, of course!

He slithered up the river bank and emerged from the water, his long, long coils glistening in the morning sun. He certainly was a fearsome sight. Even Kwaku Ananse bit his tongue in fear, but did not show it. He greeted the monster python like a brother.

'Why, thank you, thank you for appearing, Brother Python,' he said in salutation. 'You are indeed all that I said you were. Did you hear me ticking off that foolish man? You ought to have seen him run. Now come and have the meal I've brought you.'

The python was so hungry, hungry after his long sleep that he gladly swallowed all that was put before him: the powdered yam, the eggs and the calabash of good palm

wine. When the bowls and the calabash were empty, the python thanked Kwaku Ananse for the food and listened gladly, gladly to more compliments.

After a while, Kwaku Ananse said, 'Brother Python, Brother Python, I have a favour to ask you. I argued with that foolish man about your length. He said you were not even long enough to go round his hut. I said you were as long, long, long as six huts put together. Could I measure you with this log I've brought along?'

By now the python was feeling sleepy and in good temper, so he gladly consented to the strange request. He stretched himself out along the straight young tree, as Kwaku Ananse showed him. So enormous was he that even then his head poked out above one end of the log.

'Well, friend, how much do I measure?' he asked.

'Not so hasty, not so hasty,' Kwaku replied. 'I have to measure you Ashanti fashion. To be quite sure I must tie you to the log with these creepers.'

With that he took the tough twining ropes and wound them round and round the python and the log, starting at the head and ending at the tail. All the while, the crafty Kwaku Ananse counted aloud some measures and

paced carefully up and down, as if taking strict count of
the python's length. Soon the monster python was well
and truly bound.

His task accomplished, Kwaku Ananse went back to
the tree stump and brought out his axe. The python now
began to look alarmed.

'Come now, come now, friend,' the python said. 'Untie
me, untie me, these ropes are tight and the sun is very
hot. You must have my measure by now.'

'I've got your measure, all right,' laughed Ananse.

At the top of his voice, he shouted to the villagers,
calling them to come and look. When they arrived, they
could hardly believe their eyes. There was the huge, huge
python trussed up like a roasting chicken. As they
gathered round open-mouthed, Kwaku Ananse went up
to the python's tail and—swish, swish, swish—down
came the axe and off went the tail.

'That's for the first child you stole,' he said, ignoring
the python's pleas and curses.

Swish, swish, swish! Down came the axe again and
took off more pieces of python, until there was only half
his body left.

'That's for the pig you ate, that for the sheep, that for
the cow, that for the goat. . . .' continued Ananse.

14

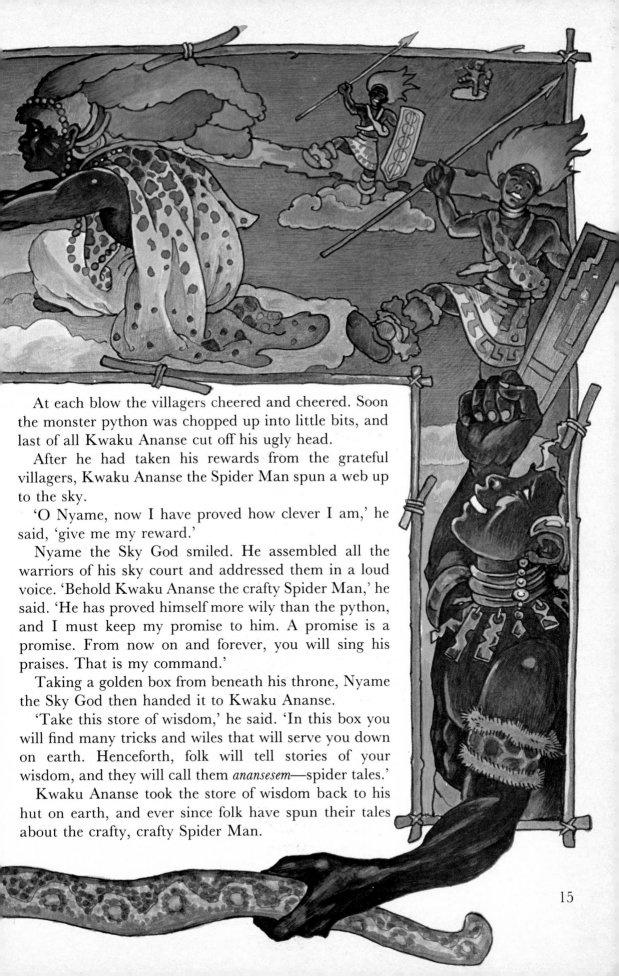

At each blow the villagers cheered and cheered. Soon the monster python was chopped up into little bits, and last of all Kwaku Ananse cut off his ugly head.

After he had taken his rewards from the grateful villagers, Kwaku Ananse the Spider Man spun a web up to the sky.

'O Nyame, now I have proved how clever I am,' he said, 'give me my reward.'

Nyame the Sky God smiled. He assembled all the warriors of his sky court and addressed them in a loud voice. 'Behold Kwaku Ananse the crafty Spider Man,' he said. 'He has proved himself more wily than the python, and I must keep my promise to him. A promise is a promise. From now on and forever, you will sing his praises. That is my command.'

Taking a golden box from beneath his throne, Nyame the Sky God then handed it to Kwaku Ananse.

'Take this store of wisdom,' he said. 'In this box you will find many tricks and wiles that will serve you down on earth. Henceforth, folk will tell stories of your wisdom, and they will call them *anansesem*—spider tales.'

Kwaku Ananse took the store of wisdom back to his hut on earth, and ever since folk have spun their tales about the crafty, crafty Spider Man.

Death's Godson

In a small Spanish village there lived a poor peasant and his wife who were blessed one day by the birth of a son. The father was so happy that he made up his mind to give the boy a very special godfather.

Without more ado, he set out in search of a godfather worthy of his son. He had not walked far when he ran into the Devil.

'Hello there, José,' said the Devil, winking at the wandering peasant. 'I hear you are seeking a godfather for your newborn son. Well, your search is over: where in the world could you find a more worthy godfather than me? I am the best there is.'

'Away with you, Satan,' said the poor man. 'I know of your devilish ways. You may be strong, but you do not know the meaning of justice and goodness. It is such qualities a poor man values most.'

At this rebuff, the Devil snorted, leapt up and down in a fury, then vanished whence he had come, his long tail between his legs.

Some time later, José's path chanced to cross that of a Saint, who stopped him and said politely, 'Ah, my son, I hear you seek a godfather for your newborn child. 'Tis true, I have no earthly riches, but I am as honest as the day is long. Would I be suitable?'

José was impressed by the Saint's kind offer, but he shook his head firmly.

'I am sorry, but you cannot help me. Your reputation is, of course, spotless, but you haven't a peseta to your name. I seek a godfather who can help my son get on in life.'

'Your words weigh heavy on my soul,' replied the Saint. 'Ambition is not always a wise companion.'

With that the Saint went on his way.

The poor peasant continued his journey. As he walked along a desolate mountain path, he suddenly came upon a gaunt figure in white blocking his way. In great dread, he recognised the solemn figure standing before him. It was Death.

Her fleshless bones were clad in a long white shroud; her gleaming eyeless skull was hooded and, in her left hand, she held a long sharp scythe.

José was terrified.

'Is my time up?' he asked aghast. 'Why do you stand across my path?'

'No,' she replied. 'Your time is not yet due. I am here because I know of your quest. You have spoken with the Devil and the Saint; and neither suit your needs. It is not a godfather you should seek, a godmother would be much more fitting. So here I am to offer you my services.'

'I am well pleased by your offer,' replied José when he had got over his shock and surprise. 'You are the very person I am looking for. You are all-powerful, for in your presence every person quakes with fear, whether he be rich or poor, great or small, young or old. Your judgement is final and your sharp scythe spares no one. You are indeed the ideal godmother for my son. The christening shall be celebrated this coming Saturday.'

The hooded skull nodded. 'You will not regret it,' came the hollow voice. 'When my godson attains the age of twenty years, he will lack for neither fame nor fortune. That I promise. You have chosen wisely. I shall attend the christening at nine o'clock precisely.'

Having found a godmother suited to his needs, José turned back and headed for home. By the time Saturday arrived, everyone in the village was talking about José's unusual choice of godparent for his son. The local priest had spent much time searching in the holy scripts for good reasons to prevent the uncommon baptism. But he found none.

Punctual as ever, Death arrived at the church on the stroke of nine. The crowded congregation gaped at her in awe, but Death paid them no heed as she walked very slowly through the church. She seemed to cast a spell of silence upon all present.

Once the ceremony was over, Death gave José a bag of gold, and said, 'When my godson reaches the age of twenty, I shall return. Then I shall bestow much honour and glory upon him.'

With that she gently touched the child upon the head with her fleshless hand, as if in blessing, caressing him with her bony fingers. The congregation watched in fear as she departed in the same sombre manner as she had come.

Time passed quickly. The months and the years flew by, and it came to the time for Death's godson to celebrate his twentieth birthday. No one had cast from their mind the promised visit of Death on that fateful day; and every member of José's household grew more

18

and more nervous as the hour of destiny drew near.

Finally, at midday, when the birthday celebrations were at their height, a window clattered open and a chill gust of wind swept into the room. Death in her white shroud appeared before them.

'Happy Birthday, Godson,' she said. 'I'm glad to see you have grown up into a strong and handsome young man, and I am exceedingly proud to be your godmother. I trust that soon you will be proud of me.'

'I am already grateful to you, Godmother,' replied the poor peasant's son. 'For, thanks to your gold, we have never lacked for anything in this house.'

'That is nothing compared with the gift I am about to grant you,' she said. 'Come with me for a moment, I wish to speak to you alone.'

The young man followed his godmother into an adjoining room and sat beside her, as she bade him.

'The time is nigh for me to fulfil my pledge,' said Death quietly. 'I promised your father that I would make you a man of means, commanding great respect. As ever, I shall keep my promise.'

Thereupon she took a sprig of some unknown herb from beneath her shroud.

'Take this magic herb,' she said. 'With its help you will become the most famous physician in all the land. When you visit someone who is sick, simply cast your gaze to the bedhead: should you see me standing by the right side, instruct the family to make a potion from this herb. In no time at all the patient will recover, no matter how grave the illness.

'However, should you see me standing on the left side of the bedhead, do not use the magic herb at any cost. The patient is fated to die and the herb cannot change this. If you try to go against my will and save someone who must die, you will bring yourself much grief.

'No matter how many times you use the herb, it will remain as fresh and potent as before. And mark this— only you will be able to see me; to all others I shall remain invisible.'

As she finished speaking, she touched her godson on the shoulder with her bony hand and left the house. He was well pleased with his gift, having complete faith in its powers, for he knew that Death always kept her word.

And so it was. The fame of the young doctor spread

rapidly throughout Spain and, in spite of his young years, he soon became the most sought-after physician in the land. He could earn as much money as he liked, and he lived the life of a rich gentleman.

It was said of him that he worked miracles—giving a potion made from a magic herb which always cured the patient within three days. But it was also whispered that if the young doctor said someone would die, then they were undoubtedly doomed.

One day Death's godson was called to the home of a very rich and influential family. The patient was the couple's only son, a three-year-old boy. Nothing pleased the doctor more than being able to cure such helpless victims of disease as young children. Full of confidence, he took up his magic herb and headed for the mansion.

Weeping inconsolably, the mother and father received him and immediately showed him into the sick room where the little boy was lying. As soon as he entered, the doctor froze with fear, for above the little, moaning form stood Death—on the left side of the bedhead. He looked at his godmother, pleading with her silently to reprieve the little child. But Death, as we all know, is pitiless. She returned his look with a cold, hard stare.

'Sir,' the mother said, as the silence lengthened ominously into minutes, 'will my little son be saved? I know that only you can give the answer.'

The doctor hesitated, looking into Death's sightless eyes. After several moments more, he firmly turned away from his godmother and said, 'Yes Senora, he will be saved. Make him a potion from this herb, and he will recover.'

The mother threw herself at his feet, overcome with gratitude and happiness. She promised to reward him with whatsoever he desired for saving her dear son's life.

'I require no reward, Senora,' he said. 'I am already a rich man. Your son's recovery is reward enough for me.'

When the young doctor arrived back home, he found it as cold and still as death. A moaning, biting wind swept every room, making his teeth chatter and his body tremble. He knew at once whom he would find there waiting for him.

His godmother was standing in the house, with a countenance terrible enough to chill the strongest heart.

'Fool!' she cried. 'How dare you disobey me! I stood

clearly on the left of the child's bed. You saw me perfectly well, yet you deliberately ignored me.'

'I am truly sorry, Godmother,' he said with downcast eyes. 'My heart bled at the thought of the child's death. Pray find it in your heart to pardon me this once.'

'I have never pardoned anyone, for I have no heart,' she said. 'Yet I do not understand this strange feeling I have for you that causes me to neglect my duties. I will forgive you just this once.'

Death's godson knelt before his godmother and kissed the hem of her shroud in gratitude. Death's lipless mouth parted in what was, perhaps, a smile.

The young doctor's fame went before him throughout Spain and one day he was summoned to the royal court where the king himself lay on his deathbed. The entire country was deeply saddened by this sickness since the king was good and just and well-liked by his subjects. Were he to die, his evil nephew, whom everybody feared and hated, would take the crown. The king had no son of his own and, since his daughter was unmarried, there was no son-in-law to inherit the kingdom.

The doctor entered the palace, where he was received by the princess and the court. Although consumed by her grief, the princess somehow felt her heart grow lighter on seeing him.

'Oh, kind sir,' she begged, 'please do all you can to save my father's life. Were he to die, the country would be doomed to misery and I should be forced to wed my evil cousin.'

Tears welled up once more in her lovely hazel eyes, overflowed and ran uncontrollably down her pallid cheeks.

Moved by the wistful beauty of the princess, the doctor gave his word to do all that was in his power. He hoped with all his heart that his godmother would not appear on the left side of the bedhead.

He was ushered into the royal bedchamber where the king lay pale and still on silken sheets. And Death stood behind him at the left.

Utterly despondent, the young doctor remained silent for several moments, pretending to examine the patient.

The princess, standing behind him, could not endure the long silence, and asked in a barely audible whisper, 'Dear sir, can you save my father?'

21

'I think not,' he replied gently, avoiding her gaze. But when he looked and saw the misery in her eyes, he continued, without realising what he was saying, 'Do not grieve, Princess. On second thoughts, your father will be saved.'

As he made his way home later that day, he walked with a heavy, fearful tread. For he knew only too well that his godmother would be waiting for him. And so she was; as he entered the house, the dank, pervasive smell of the grave assailed his nostrils and a piercing wind chilled him to the marrow.

Death was standing before a large open window, her white shroud billowing through the room, her bare skull twisted in a dreadful scowl. Even though the young man was used to death and suffering, he could not hold back a cry of horror when confronted by such a fearful sight.

'You have disobeyed me a second time,' Death hissed. 'You have cheated Death; no one has dared to do that before. Now you must be punished as you deserve.'

'No, Godmother, I beg of you,' cried the young man. 'What I did was wrong, I know. But I did it to save the country and the princess. She is so beautiful, gentle and kind, and her cousin whom she must wed, should her father die, is a loathsome creature. I disobeyed you to bring happiness to others. Please forgive me.'

'Mortal feelings mean nothing to me,' Death said. 'What must be must be; you cannot alter that. However, I understand that what you did was not for yourself, so I shall forgive you a second time. But mark my words well: there will be no third pardon. Should you cross me a third time, you shall suffer the fate of the one you try to save.'

Two years passed by. In the meantime, the doctor was appointed Court Physician and personal adviser to the King of Spain. There was no one in the entire kingdom more highly esteemed than he. Yet what pleased the young man most was not the honours he received, nor the fame he had acquired. What pleased him most was the love he knew the princess had for him and he for her. The king grew to trust him well and, given time, they hoped he would permit his daughter to wed the poor peasant's son.

However, one day the princess fell ill and had to take to her bed. During the night she became much worse and

the doctor was called to see her early the following morning. He entered the bedroom in great dread, for he knew that if his godmother were at the left side of the bedhead he could do nothing.

The lace curtains that had draped the royal four-poster bed were now drawn right back to give more light and there—Oh horror!—was Death standing on the left. Her sightless eye sockets stared defiantly at her godson.

Upon seeing her beloved, the princess smiled weakly. 'I knew you would come,' she said with a sigh. 'I feel much better now because I know I am safe in your hands.'

His eyes moist with tears, he avoided her gaze and ordered a potion to be prepared with the magic herb. He

dared not look in the direction of his godmother who stood there pointing a condemning finger at him.

Bending over his beloved princess, he whispered, 'You have nothing to fear, my true love.'

When he returned to his house towards dusk, a damp, bone-chilling wind lashed his face as soon as he crossed the threshold. His godmother, standing gaunt and tall and white before him, stared at him mournfully without uttering a sound. Was it fancy, or were there tears glistening in her empty eye-sockets?

'I cannot be angry with you, my godson, for there is nothing I can do to save you now. Come with me; I have something to show you.'

The young man followed Death across valleys and meadows as in a dream, and he presently found himself in a mysterious valley filled with white boulders and bare stones. Not a single blade of grass, not a flower, not a shrub or tree grew there.

'Come,' said Death beckoning him on, 'I shall show you something that no one else has ever seen.'

Death's godson followed her numbly into an enormous cavern. The floor was covered with thousands upon thousands of lighted candles of all sizes.

'What are these candles, Godmother?' he enquired.

'Each candle represents a human life, my godson,' she said. 'The very tall ones are the lives of the newborn; the medium-sized ones are those of folk in middle years; and the shortest ones are those of the old and ailing.'

Death stopped suddenly before a candle whose feeble flame was flickering weakly.

'Godmother,' said the doctor, 'whose flame of life is that?'

'It is the flame of your beloved princess, and it must soon go out. I cannot prevent her death.'

Death's godson looked in sadness at his godmother as she went on, 'I can but offer you, my only godson, the fate which must befall all men at some time or another. I am the sole possessor of the dreadful power which enables me to unite you with your loved one. Death will not keep you apart. I shall extinguish your flame as well. That will be my final gift to you.'

Her icy breath filled the cave.

At once Death's godson fell down at her feet as the two candles flickered and died together.

25

The Man Who Sold Words

In times gone by there lived in ancient China a man named Lo Shi, who was neither dull nor bright. From early morning till late at night he toiled for others, scraped together a little money and, when the time was ripe, took himself a wife. Then, after he had earned himself a little more money, he went off with a party of merchants to trade in a distant town by the Great Wall.

Lo Shi and the merchants journeyed many days, finally arrived, unloaded their wares and began to trade. It was not long before Lo Shi had sold all he had—for he had not much at all. With the proceeds he purchased a little of this, even less of that, counted out his change and found he still had twenty coins remaining.

'Perhaps I could buy my wife a present with the money,' he pondered. 'That would please her.'

So off he went to the bazaar where he came upon an old white-bearded man crying, 'Words for sale! Words for sale!'

Lo Shi was curious and asked, 'What sort of words are you selling?'

'Words that are spoken,' the man replied.

'Then let's hear your words,' said Lo Shi.

'For the price of twenty coins I'll gladly tell you,' said the man.

'Perhaps they truly are fine words,' thought Lo Shi. He was sorry to give up all his coins and not buy his wife a present, but he badly wished to hear what the old sage had to say.

So he looked at the old man and said, 'Here you are then, old man, twenty coins—now speak.'

The white-bearded man took the coins, stared hard at Lo Shi and said these words:

'Beware of an inn in a valley.
Take no shelter from the rain.
Harken well to a wayfarer's tale.
Wash not your head that's damp with oil.
Learn these words and tell them to Chou Win:
Ee du gootsai, san shin me
(One du of grain, three shins of rice).'

Lo Shi returned to the party of merchants, his head still ringing with the strange words. Next day, the party set off on their return journey. By evening they had come to an inn that stood in a valley at the foot of a tall hill.

27

The merchants all took rooms for the night in this inn, but Lo Shi, when he saw that the inn stood in a valley remembered the first warning of the old sage. Unnoticed by the others he therefore left the inn, climbed to the top of the hill overlooking the valley and prepared to spend the night there.

At midnight Lo Shi was awoken by a loud rumbling. He looked across the valley and saw that a great torrent of water was rushing towards the inn. Hardly had he time to realise what was happening than the torrent had filled the valley completely.

In the morning, when he awoke and stared down into the valley not a trace of the inn remained. Nothing could be seen but a vast lake on the surface of which floated the bodies of all the drowned merchants with their wares. Lo Shi quickly loaded up his mule and left that ill-fated valley far behind.

Later that day he encountered a man who was going his way. They fell in together and continued the journey in each other's company. But they had not gone far when the sky suddenly clouded over and rain began to fall heavily. The stranger at once proposed that they take shelter from the deluge, but Lo Shi recalled the second warning of the sage and carried on alone.

Meanwhile, the stranger sheltered under an overhanging rock to avoid the rain. Lo Shi had not taken a hundred paces farther when a great crashing sound caused him to glance back. To his horror he saw that the overhanging rock had fallen and crushed the poor stranger. Lo Shi hastily moved on.

It was not long before he came to a town. In this town his cousin lived and worked at the potter's trade. Lo Shi sought out his cousin's house and that distant relative made as if to welcome the unexpected guest. However, when Lo Shi was sound asleep, the cousin fell to thinking cruel thoughts. Of late his business had not been doing well and he saw Lo Shi's visit as an opportunity to change this.

'In ancient times,' the cousin said to his wife, 'it was said that a human sacrifice had to be made in the potter's oven before it did good work. Maybe that is why our oven works so poorly. Let us send Lo Shi to the potter's workshop with food for the workers on the morrow; I'll instruct them to seize and cast into the oven the man who brings them food. That should help our business prosper.'

Next day, as the wife was cooking the dinner, she said to Lo Shi, 'Be so kind, dear cousin, as to take dinners to our workmen at the pottery.'

Being eager to please, Lo Shi readily agreed and hung the yoke over his shoulders with two baskets of food at each side. He had not covered half the distance to the pottery when he came upon a crowd at the roadside, listening to the stories of an old wayfarer. At once Lo Shi remembered the third instruction of the sage and sat down to listen to the story. While he sat there his cousin's eldest son chanced to pass and, seeing his uncle engrossed in the tale, offered to take the men their dinners himself. Lo Shi was pleased to agree.

Of course, as soon as the young man entered the pottery the workmen went to seize him, as their master had commanded. Seeing their master's son, they hesitated. However, fear got the better of them: they were much frightened of their master's wrath should they disobey him. So they took the lad and threw him into the oven.

Lo Shi meantime heard out the story and returned home, blissfully unaware of anything untoward. When his cousin and his cousin's wife caught sight of him, they were greatly amazed, though they tried not to show it.

'Did you take the men their dinners?' asked the cousin.

Lo Shi started to explain, saying, 'When I had gone half way I saw an old storyteller. He was telling such an interesting story that I stopped to listen. As I was sitting there, my nephew, your son, came along . . .'

At that, the cousin and his wife let out loud groans, causing Lo Shi to halt his story.

'Whatever is the matter?' he asked in surprise.

For several moments the two were silent, then the cousin urged Lo Shi to continue.

'Your eldest son saw how keen I was to hear out the tale, so he kindly offered to take the dinners to your workmen himself. I handed him the yoke and off he went. Is he not back yet?' asked Lo Shi.

No one answered. Lo Shi sat for a while before thanking his cousin for his hospitality and continuing his journey.

He travelled all through the night, and next day,

towards nightfall, arrived at his home.

Now, in the meantime, Lo Shi's wife, having had no news from her husband, had taken a lodger from among a gang of robbers. At that very moment when Lo Shi knocked at the gates she was sitting at home having supper with the robber. Straightaway she recognised her husband's voice, and hid the robber, but in her haste forgot to clear the rice bowls from the table.

When she had let her husband in and greeted him as a dutiful wife is obliged to do, she sat him down at the table and brought some tea. Lo Shi noticed the two pairs of chopsticks and two rice bowls already on the table.

'Why are there two pairs of chopsticks and two bowls of rice if you were here alone?' he asked his wife suspiciously.

'What an ungrateful man you are,' his wife shouted back. 'All the time you've been away I've thought of no one but you. Each evening I laid the table for two to remind me of you, just as if you were sitting here with me.'

Lo Shi said nothing. He drank his tea and finished the food in the bowl from which the robber had just been eating. After his meal, he lay down and was soon fast asleep. His wife meanwhile proceeded with her sewing in the light of the oil lamp, but being nervous she knocked over the lamp as she rose to go to bed, spilling some oil on Lo Shi's head.

The hot oil made him jump up at once. But being as clever as she was deceitful, the wife calmed him down and offered to wash the oil out of her husband's hair even at that late hour. It was then that Lo Shi recalled the fourth warning of the old sage and declined his wife's offer.

They turned out the lamp and lay down to sleep. It was at that moment the robber decided to leave his hiding place, a sharp dagger in his hand. His plan was to slit the throat of Lo Shi; thus all the host's belongings could be shared out between the wife and himself.

However, in the darkness the robber could not make out exactly where Lo Shi and his wife were lying. Then he had an idea.

'I know,' he said to himself, 'women put oil on their hair, men do not.'

He felt one head and as the hair was oily, he quickly

cut the throat of the other sleeper. Instead, therefore, of
slitting the throat of Lo Shi, he mistakenly slit the throat
of Lo Shi's wife.

In the morning, when Lo Shi awoke from his innocent
slumbers, he saw with horror the dead body of his wife,
her throat slit from ear to ear. Rushing from the house,
he called his neighbours and told them what had
happened. But the neighbours pointed an accusing finger
at poor Lo Shi, believing him to be the murderer of his
wife.

All this was reported to the district governor who sent
his guards to apprehend the bewildered Lo Shi. In no
time at all he found himself dragged before the governor,
Chou Win.

'Speak up, you rogue,' shouted Chou Win. 'Why did
you kill your wife?'

As soon as Lo Shi had learned the governor's name, he remembered the fifth instruction of the old sage. Now he fell on his knees before Chou Win and began his story.

'Most honourable lord, I went to the Great Wall to trade and before my return purchased words from a white-bearded old sage for twenty coins.'

'What sort of words did the old man sell you?' asked the governor.

Lo Shi repeated the five instructions:

'Beware of an inn in a valley.
Take no shelter from the rain.
Harken well to a wayfarer's tale.
Wash not your head that's damp with oil.
Learn these words and tell them to Chou Win:
Ee du gootsai, san shin me
(One du of grain, three shins of rice).'

The governor set to thinking, then asked, 'And did the words of the sage come true?'

'All of them except the last,' replied Lo Shi.

Chou Win again was lost in thought.

'That old sage was undoubtedly an immortal shin san,' he said at last. 'This business needs looking into

very carefully. So all the words came true except the last: ee du gootsai, san shin me. Let me think: Du Goo—that could be someone's name, and Me San too.'

The governor called in his guards and asked them whether two men by the names of Du Goo and Me San lived in the district. The guards replied that there were, indeed, two such people; they earned their living by robbing and pestering poor people. At once the guards were sent to arrest the pair and bring them to the governor.

When the frightened brigands were dragged before the governor, they straightaway owned up to all their crimes. They told him how they had made friends with Lo Shi's wife and plotted with her to rob Lo Shi of his home and fortune. But one of them had slit her throat in error.

In his anger, the governor sentenced the worthless pair to death. When the guards had led them out, Chou Win turned to Lo Shi and said, 'Now I know you have a simple heart. You are a good man. Go back to your home and find yourself a wife worthy of your devotion.'

Lo Shi thanked the governor and returned home. Before a month was out, he did indeed find himself a worthy wife, a girl poor and humble like himself. Together they lived in modesty and harmony to a venerable old age.

The Selkie Wife

Jock Guthrie lived alone on a small farm that stood above the sea in the Highlands of Scotland. He dug and he sowed and he laboured all the hours of daylight to make the two ends meet; yet he remained just as poor as a corrie crisosag—a wizened old beetle. He never even had time to take a wife.

'Och, there's nae enough food to keep a body. I canna manage twa of them,' he would say.

It was not that he was a mean soul, or that he did not wish for company. But finer feelings were hard to nurture in the stony soil of Highland farming and Jock was a bluff, straightforward fellow who did not have much time for romancing.

One warm evening in late summer, Jock went down the cliff path to the seashore to take a clearer look at the weather. The distant sunset glowed a pinkish orange and the sea reflected the colours in its calm surface.

Jock sat upon a dry rock, musing, his chin cupped in his horny hands, gazing out to sea. Suddenly, in the

midst of his thoughts, he was surprised to hear snatches of song, girlish laughter and low cheery voices. The sounds seemed to be coming from the seaward side of the rocks, at the far end of the shore.

That was odd. It was a lonely deserted spot where not a living soul was seen from one year to the next, where naught but timid rabbits scuttled over the pale sand. So now Jock approached the bay with rising curiosity. He clambered up the landward side of the rocks and peered cautiously over to the strand beyond.

The sight that met his gaze made him catch his breath in sheer astonishment. For there below him on a rocky shelf, just above the water's edge, he saw a group of young men and maidens as naked as the sun-splashed rocks. How handsome they were! Never in all his years had he cast eyes on such lovely faces, such smooth skins and such graceful limbs.

'Selkies! That's what they are,' he murmured to himself.

He'd heard stories of the selkies or seal folk who sometimes came ashore, cast aside their seal skins and played their happy games.

'Aye, I ken who y'are,' thought Jock, seeing their skins upon a nearby rock. 'And what if I take a skin for masel'?' he thought. 'It'd keep ma bed warm or be a plaid for ma back.'

Thereupon, he climbed down the rocks without being seen, dashed across the sand and snatched up a silvery skin before any of the selkies could move.

What a commotion arose when they saw him! Each lovely creature made a rush for the rock to seize a skin; then, diving in frantic haste into the sea, they swam away as fast as they were able, pulling on their seal skins as they went.

In the meantime, Jock made good his escape with the selkie skin underneath his arm. He climbed back over the rocks and crossed the dry sand towards the cliff path. However, he had not gone far when he heard footsteps padding after him over the sand and the sound of a maid softly weeping. As he turned, he saw a lovely girl holding out her hands towards him; big crystal tears were tumbling down her smooth white cheeks.

'Bide awhile, meester, I beg o' ye,' she cried. 'Hae pity on a poor wee lassie and gie me back ma selkie skin.'

Jock's heart was moved by her sobbing pleas. Yet even more his heart was pierced by a strange feeling he had never had before. Could it be that Jock the lonely farmer, who had spurned all womenfolk before, was now in love? His heart certainly felt mighty queer and he knew that he did not want to lose his new-found lassie. Not for anything.

'I dinna intend to return yon selkie skin,' he said. 'Y'll nae be awa to sea again, ma bonnie lass. Y'll stay wi' me and be ma goodwife.'

He put his plaid around the weeping maid and took her by the hand, leading her to his farm. Once there he wrapped her in a woollen blanket and gave her a supper of bannock cakes and hot brose porridge. While she was eating, he stole out to the barn, folded up her selkie skin and hid it on a beam beneath the roof, where she would never find it.

Poor maid. After her supper she lay down upon a bed and wept the whole night through. Likewise the next day too. And through the week.

But there came a time when her tears dried up and there was nothing for it but to make the best of her new mortal life. Her goodman was fairly kind to her, if a mite unpolished in his ways. He provided enough to eat and taught her all a farmer's wife should know. Though she did not love him, nor altogether accept her homely life, she did not suffer hunger, cold or beatings.

As the years went by, she bore him half a dozen children: three boys and three girls, all as handsome as can be, with large gentle brown eyes and smooth white skin, akin their mother, and strong-boned limbs and sturdy bodies, akin their father.

Although she was fond of her children and never more spoke about her life as a seal, the selkie wife cast many a sad, yearning glance towards the sea. Of an evening, when the day's work was done, she would sit upon the sandy shore, gazing sadly out to sea, as if searching for someone amid the waves. At such moments, she would sing haunting, mournful, oddly-beautiful songs that touched the heart and blurred the eye of all who chanced to catch their music on the wind.

Now it happened one time, in an evening in late spring, when the farmer had taken the three sons fishing in their boat, and the two eldest girls had gone to gather cockles in the wet sand laid bare by the ebbing tide, that the selkie wife and her youngest daughter were sitting at home.

No sooner had her husband and the other children left the house than the selkie wife was in and out of all the cupboards, feeling all along the lofty shelves, peering under beds and tables, rummaging in all the chests and boxes, sighing all the while.

'Whist, Mam,' her little daughter said, 'what is it that ye're seeking?'

'Och, ma peerie bairn,' the seal wife said, 'I'm looking for a bonnie selkie skin your father once brought hame.'

'Wad it be soft and silvery wi' bonnie bruin spots?' the daughter asked.

'Aye, ma bonnie bairn, that it wad! D'ye ken where t'is?' the selkie wife cried excitedly.

37

'That I do,' the daughter said. 'One evening as ye were down singing on the sands and I was in the old stane barn playing, I saw father come in and take doon such a bonnie skin from a wooden beam. He didna ken that I was there. How he sighed as he stroked that skin and held it to his cheek. Then he stood on tiptoe and put it back upon the roof beam.'

The girl had hardly finished speaking when her mother rushed from the house towards the old stone barn. In an instant she was inside the barn, standing on a box, feeling with trembling hands along the beams. She felt all the way along one rough wooden beam, and then another and another. At last, as her dusty, excited fingers edged along a beam they touched something soft—her selkie skin! Pulling it down, she clasped it lovingly to her breast and ran back with it to the house.

'Fare ye well, ma bonnie bairn,' she said to her little daughter. 'I must awa to ma ain hame.'

She ran across the heather to the cliff, clutching the seal skin close like some very precious thing. Down the cliff path she hurried to the sea, pulled on her long-lost skin and, with a last wave to her two daughters on the shore, she dived into the water and swam away.

When she was already far out to sea, she saw the fishing boat with her husband and three sons. For several moments she swam alongside it as if trying to tell the fishermen something. They were puzzled by the friendly seal that swam so close, its head lifted above the waves, looking at them with its lovely gentle eyes shining with a gleam that mingled joy with sadness. All of a sudden, with a painful cry of recognition, Jock Guthrie snatched up his net and went to cast it in the water.

But it was too late. The seal had dived under the

waves and was soon far, far away, swimming out to sea.
That was the last Jock Guthrie ever saw of his beloved
selkie wife.

In the months and years that followed, Jock would
often wander of an evening, when his day's work was
done, upon the sandy shore. Or he would sit upon a rock
gazing hopefully out to sea. But never again did he catch
a glimpse of his bonnie wee selkie. She had gone where
no mortal man could ever follow.

Scarface

Early one morning, as the Sun rose from his bed beyond the Rocky Mountains, his handsome son Morning Star addressed him boldly.

'Father, I am tired of my lonely vigil in the sky. I wish to take a wife to keep me company.'

'Have you chosen a bride?' asked the Sun.

'I have looked down upon the tepees of the Blackfeet tribe and seen there a beautiful Indian maid called Soatsaki,' Morning Star replied. 'I love her dearly and would ask her to be my wife.'

His father shook his head. 'You cannot wed an earthly maid, my son,' he said. 'She would bring unhappiness to you and to herself. Her rightful home is on the earth. Should she dwell in our kingdom in the skies she would sorely miss her people.'

Morning Star was very sad. He could not put thoughts of the enchanting Indian girl from his mind. From his lofty home he gazed down each dawn upon her as she slept within her father's tepee. His longing grew and soon touched the heart of his mother, the pale Moon. She begged the Sun to change his mind.

At last the Sun reluctantly gave permission.

'But hear me well,' he said to Morning Star. 'Once she dwells within our realm she must never again look upon the Blackfeet tepees, lest her heart be filled with longing to return.'

Morning Star was overjoyed. He painted his bronze body, stuck a red eagle's feather in his black hair, and put on his scarlet cloak and shining black moccasins. Dressed thus, he appeared before the maid he loved so dearly. Though she was startled to see the handsome stranger, she was quickly taken by his noble bearing and fell in love with him. Gladly she agreed to be his wife.

'Dear Soatsaki,' said the handsome brave, 'to marry me you must give up your earthly life. My tepee is in the skies. You must bid farewell to the people of your tribe forever.'

So in love was Soatsaki that she readily consented to what he said. After parting with her family, she flew up to her new home in the heavens with her husband, Morning Star.

The young brave and his squaw were very happy and, in the space of several moons, a son was born. They called him Little Star.

One day, as Soatsaki sat in the Moon's tepee nursing her infant son, she asked the Moon why it was that the big iron pot in the centre of their home always boiled without a fire.

'That is because it has a magic source of heat beneath it,' said the Moon. 'But heed my words, daughter of the earth, you must never move the pot. If you do, great misfortune will befall you.'

Soatsaki thanked her mother-in-law for her warning and gave her word she would not touch the pot.

Yet at midday, when pale Moon was sleeping soundly, the lovely Indian maid could not still her curiosity. She approached the empty pot and tried to pull it to one side. She tugged and pushed until finally, with one great heave, she shifted it aside.

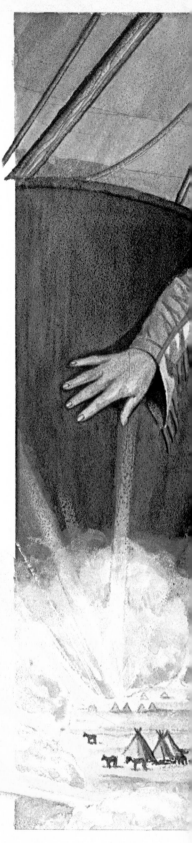

Imagine her surprise when she discovered what was
below: she could see right through the hole beneath the
pot! As she knelt down to take a better look, she saw her
former home below upon the silent plains. She could see
the green edge of the prairie with its shooting threads of
gold, scarlet and blue, the blossoming wolf willow and
dog rose. Her heart beat wildly as she recognised the
tepee clusters of her own Blackfeet tribe. And she was
filled with an uncontrollable longing to see her kinsfolk
once again.

When her husband Morning Star returned, he noticed
at once the downcast look upon his wife's lovely face and
asked her for the reason.

'If only I could see my people once again,' she said, 'I
should be very happy. Though I am content here with
you, my husband, and our infant son, I long to pay just
one visit to my native land.'

Morning Star was hurt at these words, for he knew
that his wife had broken her promise.

When his father, the Sun, heard the news, he flew into
a rage.

'You are unworthy of a place in our heavens,' he
shouted at her. 'Go then back to earth from whence you

43

came. And take your papoose with you. No more will you see your husband, Morning Star. That shall be a punishment for your disobedience.'

Soatsaki and Little Star were wrapped up tightly in a caribou skin and lowered on a leather thong through the hole beneath the iron pot. But before they reached the earth, Little Star began to cry and forced his head out of the caribou skin. As he did so, the leather thong slid along his face leaving a deep cut, two fingers' length across.

In the course of time, his face wound healed, though it left an ugly scar down one side of his face. So disfigured was he that the other braves of the tribe gave him the name of Poia, meaning Scarface. Even though he was daring and skilful in hunting and battle, bringing much glory to his tribe, the braves and maidens shunned him. Even the little children taunted him as he passed by, calling, 'There goes Scarface, the ugly one!'

Meanwhile, his poor mother, Soatsaki, pined away for her lost husband and finally died of a broken heart, leaving her son all by himself. He grew up with no family or friends for company. He walked alone.

The lonely years passed by and when he came to manhood, Poia fell in love with the daughter of a neighbouring chief. She much admired his skill with bow and arrow and she deeply respected his strength in combat with the other braves. However, she could not gaze upon his scarred, disfigured face without a shudder of disgust. So she refused him.

It was rare indeed for an Indian maid to refuse a brave's proposal. And Poia was greatly hurt and much ashamed. He could not show his face before the tribe without their scorn.

'I must find a way of reaching my grandfather, the Sun,' thought Scarface in his misery. 'Perhaps he will take pity on me and remove this blemish from my face.'

So he set out on a journey westwards towards the lofty snow-capped mountains. For many moons he walked, climbing the jagged peaks, crossing the swift rolling rivers, leaping over the moving ice floes, until finally he reached the end of the world where the mighty waters meet the sky.

He sat down exhausted on the rocky shore and looked up at the Sun.

45

'O Mighty Sun,' he cried, 'Father of my father, grandfather to Little Star. Hear me now, I pray thee. Show me a way up to the heavens, that I may come to seek your aid. My soul is troubled. I would rather go to the land of the spirits than live on earth, bearing forever the name of Scarface.'

For three days and nights, Scarface waited, never eating, never drinking. On the fourth day, just as dawn was breaking, he opened his eyes to see a path of light stretching before him. It led from where he sat right across the waters to the sky.

Great was his joy as he stepped upon the firm broad stairway and mounted it with fast-beating heart into the heavens.

But then, just as he reached the home where he was born, he saw some way off seven giant eagles attacking his dear father Morning Star. In another moment they would surely have pecked out his eyes. Swiftly taking arrows from his quiver, he fitted them into his bow, one after the other, and shot all seven eagles. Morning Star was overjoyed to see his long-lost son and rushed to join him.

'You have passed the trial of courage, my son,' he said. 'Now I can take you to your grandfather the Sun.'

Mighty Sun did indeed take pity on his grandson and removed the ugly scar.

'From this time forth,' he said, 'no one will call you Poia. And since you have borne your ugliness so bravely, I shall reward you with this magic flute. It will charm the heart of all who hear its music. Return to earth, my grandson, and wed the maiden whom you love. Then, should you so desire, you may return with her to your birthplace in the skies.'

So Little Star, for such he had become again, went back to the plains and stood before the great tepee of the neighbouring chief. As soon as he played his flute, the chief's lovely daughter emerged enchanted, and fell deeply in love with the now handsome brave.

They were soon married and after the wedding celebrations they went hand in hand to the sky abode of the Sun, the Moon and Morning Star. And there they remain to this very day. If you look up at the evening sky, you can sometimes see the tepees of their many children in what some folk call the Milky Way.

The Beauty of Life

In Georgia, in the olden times, there lived a wise and noble woman, Queen Magdana, who ruled her rich, green land justly. When her husband died her son Rostomel became the sole love of her life. She loved him more than my words can convey, and fondly watched the tender, callow youth grow to sturdy manhood. And it was not only she who thought him more handsome than all others.

Yet as the days passed into years, she began to notice a cloud upon his handsome brow. For no apparent reason, the young man turned taciturn and gloomy. No wild gallops over the green hills of Georgia, no wistful songs, no passionate black-eyed glances from maidens dancing, could drive away his black moods or lift the gloom.

Pensive and downcast, he would take his burden into a distant corner of the palace grounds and give himself up to his melancholy daydreams. At last, the good queen could bear her son's sadness no longer.

49

'O my son,' she said, 'tell me what painful thoughts are gnawing at your heart, what sorrows drive the smile from your lips.'

'Mother mine,' the prince replied, 'I would ask you in return to answer me one question: where is my father?'

'Your father?' replied the queen surprised. 'Why, he died a long time ago.'

'Died? What does that mean?' asked the prince.

'Know, my son,' said the queen, 'that we all come from the earth and one day must return there. The time will come when good Mother Earth will take us back into her womb. That, my son, is what it means to die.'

'I do not understand,' her son replied. 'Surely God who granted us life did not do so just to take it back again? No, that cannot be. There must be on earth a place where eternal life exists and people know no death. I shall go in search of that place to seek immortality. Dear Mother, pray forgive me for leaving you but should I stay I would surely die from my sorrow.'

In vain did his poor mother beg him to remain with her; in vain did she shed bitter tears; in vain did she waste away in her grief. Her son did not surrender to her entreaties. One day he embraced her and went on his way in search of eternal life.

For a long, long time the prince wandered through the world and visited many lands, yet nowhere did he find a land of immortality. Then one day he came to a silent, treeless plain. As he gazed into the distance he saw against a clear, blue sky, a deer standing motionless, its horns held high.

As he approached, the deer asked Rostomel, 'Young man, what is it you seek in this barren land?'

'I seek a land of immortality,' the prince replied.

'Immortality? There is no such thing,' said the deer. 'But look, do you see above us the boundless blue skies? It is my destiny to stand here motionless in this plain until my horns reach the sky. Will you stay here with me until that distant time? For all those years, I pledge, you will be immortal. Only when my earthly assignment is complete will you die.'

'Oh no,' replied the prince. 'Even hundreds of centuries are not immortality. And I want to be immortal. So farewell, my friend.'

On he went until eventually he came to a line of barren

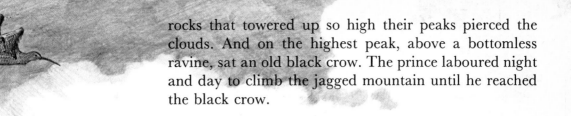

rocks that towered up so high their peaks pierced the clouds. And on the highest peak, above a bottomless ravine, sat an old black crow. The prince laboured night and day to climb the jagged mountain until he reached the black crow.

'Why have you come?' the crow asked him. 'What do you seek on this godforsaken mountain?'

'Immortality,' the young man replied.

'Immortality? There is no such thing,' said the crow. 'Just look down into this bottomless ravine that lies below me. It is my hapless fate to remain here until I've pecked away each grain of sand, each piece of grit from this mountain and completely filled the ravine. You are welcome to remain with me down the ages until my task is complete. For all that time you will be immortal, that I promise you.'

'Oh no,' said the prince. 'What are long centuries to me? I seek only immortality and I shall one day find it. Farewell.'

Once again he turned his footsteps into the unknown. After many, many leagues he came at last to the very edge of the world. Beneath a glorious rainbow an endless, marvellous ocean stretched before him. Transparent blue waves capped with trembling, snow-white foam splashed upon the sandy shore and lapped gently at his feet. And there in the boundless distance, far, far beyond that rainbow's end, through a golden, pinkish haze, was shining a wondrous divine light. It seemed to be beckoning to Rostomel. It caressed his soul, excited his heart and enticed him towards it.

In an instant the enraptured prince was transported to the other shore. He found himself in a glittering, shining palace—and there before him, radiant in the light of a myriad precious stones, he beheld the most beautiful maiden he had ever seen.

Who she was he did not know. But even the stars and the rays of the sun faded before her bright beauty. Her voice came to him like the gentle rustle of velvet upon a silken couch.

'Welcome, Rostomel, to my eternal realm. I was born on the first day of creation and I shall remain here until the end of time. As long as you stay with me, renouncing all worldly life, death cannot touch you. You will be immortal. For I am the Beauty of Life.'

Rostomel gladly remained. A millennium passed and he, never tiring of her beauty, did not take his eyes from the wonderful face.

More centuries went by. But gradually down the ages his heart began to ache, and one day he said to the

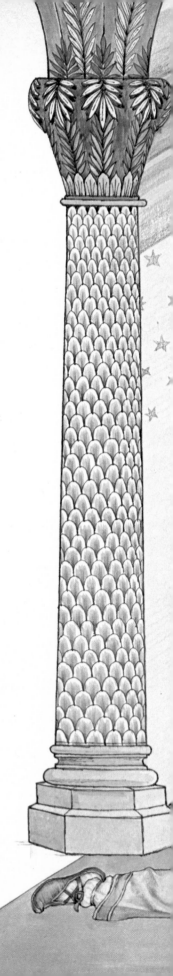

beautiful goddess, 'Divine Beauty, how many years have passed since I last saw my dear mother and the green hills and valleys of my native Georgia?'

'Ah, I perceive,' said Beauty, 'that Mother Earth will not easily surrender what is rightly hers. Go then, bow down before the universal law, yield to human destiny. But take this gift in memory of me: two flowers, one purple and one milk-white.

'If you wish to live your life again on earth, to experience the years you've lost contemplating my beauty, just sniff the purple flower. Should you come to understand the beauty of death, bring the milk-white flower to your nose and inhale its fragrance deeply.'

Having said farewell to the divine Beauty of Life, Rostomel went back the way he had come. On his journey home he observed the familiar mountain and on its summit still sat the old black crow. He called to it but no answer came. As he climbed closer to the crow, he touched it with his hand and at once its body crumbled into dust. Looking down, Rostomel now saw no sign of the deep ravine—it was filled to the brim with sand and grit from the mountain. That old crow had fulfilled its earthly assignment and gained eternal peace.

Rostomel went farther and came to the silent plain where the deer had stood. All that now remained were a white breastbone and sun-bleached skull from which two horns reached up through the clouds into the domed canopy of the heavens. Like the crow, the deer too had completed its assignment and merited eternal sleep.

Finally, Rostomel arrived back in his native Georgia. But what now did he see? He could not recognise a single person or a single thing. Where a wilderness once stood, villages and bustling towns now thrived. Unfamiliar people in unfamiliar dress speaking a strange tongue walked the land, and he could not understand their words. Yet there were the familiar mountains where he had first seen light of day, where he had grown up, where he had abandoned his dear mother.

Where then was she? Where was the castle in which Queen Magdana lived and ruled her valiant people? All now was wasteland, all was as silent as the grave, and only the slabs of moss-covered stones were silent witnesses to the once-great palace.

As he drew closer, he saw with fast-beating heart the

54

ancient watchtower still standing tall and straight upon the hill where fountains once played, where sweet songs resounded and where maidenly feet once trod the grass.

He ran towards the watchtower and came upon an ancient elder bent down by the burden of his years. The old man was sitting on a gravestone murmuring the words of a prayer through trembling lips.

'Tell me, holy father,' said Rostomel in his haste interrupting the man's prayers, 'is this not the place where once lived Magdana, the great and glorious queen who ruled her people so justly? I am her son, heir to the throne. If my mother is no longer living then I am now your king and sovereign.'

'Magdana? Magdana?' the old man repeated. 'I scarcely understand your words, young man; you do not speak our language. Your words are those of the ancient chronicles. I once studied them and therefore recognise some of your speech. Magdana, you say? Yes, there is a legend—I know not whether it is true—that a great queen lived here over a thousand years ago or more. As I recall, her name was Magdana. She had a son, or so the legend goes, who went away and disappeared without a trace. Magdana died of a broken heart, and her kingdom soon perished with her.'

Prince Rostomel was silent for a long time, tears of anguish all the while coursing down his cheeks.

All last, he raised his moist face to the heavens and cried, 'O eternal secret of time! What am I now? Nothing more than a forgotten legend?'

Thereupon, he took out his purple flower, put it to his nose and breathed in its fragrant scent. Instantly he aged; he became an old man, weak and bent; his keen eyes turned dull, his bronzed skin became dried and parched over ancient bones. No longer did he have the strength even to lift his hand to the pocket where he kept the milk-white flower.

In a hoarse whisper he appealed to the old priest, 'Quick, father, take out my milk-white flower and put it to my nose, that I might inhale its fragrance and finally know the mysterious delight of death.'

Rostomel died. The people came and returned him to the earth from which he came, and no one has ever disturbed his sleep. But on his grave there grow each year two flowers—one purple, one milk-white.

55

Six Blind Men and an Elephant

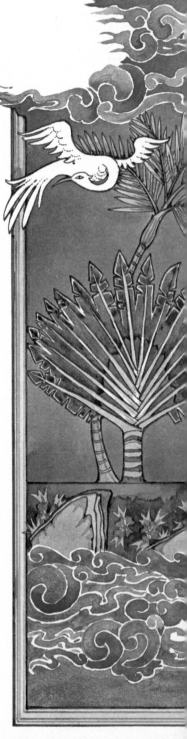

A long time ago in the valley of the Brahmaputra River in India there lived six men who were much inclined to boast of their wit and learning. Though they were no longer young and had all been blind since birth, they would compete with one another to see who could tell the tallest story.

Every evening, when the sun was setting behind the palms, and the air was full of wood smoke and spices, one of the old men would begin a new story. It might be of how he had spoken with Lord Krishna, whom he had met—or so he said—while walking in the forest. The man would tell how Lord Krishna appeared in a dazzling blue glow, playing a merry, enchanting tune upon his flute. And he would tell how Lord Krishna had granted him eternal wisdom above all other mortals.

The second blind man might tell of the bulbul bird, who received his brilliant crimson breast one day when he espied the tiger fleeing from the porcupine. So funny was the scene that the bird had burst himself laughing and the blood had spilled all over his breast.

Not to be outdone, the third blind man would cough and clack his tongue as if holding a conversation with a lizard on a mud hut wall. Having taken inspiration thus, he might tell of the times of good King Vikra Maditya who had saved a brahmin's child and wed a humble peasant girl.

After him the fourth, followed by the fifth and then the sixth would tell their stories, each more fantastic than the one before. So it continued, the blind men passing away the time in harmless boasting.

One day, however, they fell to arguing. The object of their dispute was the elephant. Now, since each was blind, none had ever seen that mighty beast of whom so many tales are told. So, to satisfy their minds and settle the dispute, they decided to go and seek out an elephant.

Having hired a young guide, Dookiram by name, they
set out early one morning in single file along the forest
track, each placing his hands on the back of the man in
front. It was not long before they came to a forest
clearing where a huge bull elephant, quite tame, was
standing contemplating his menu for the day.

The six blind men became quite excited; at last they
would satisfy their minds. Thus it was that the men took
turns to investigate the elephant's shape and form.

57

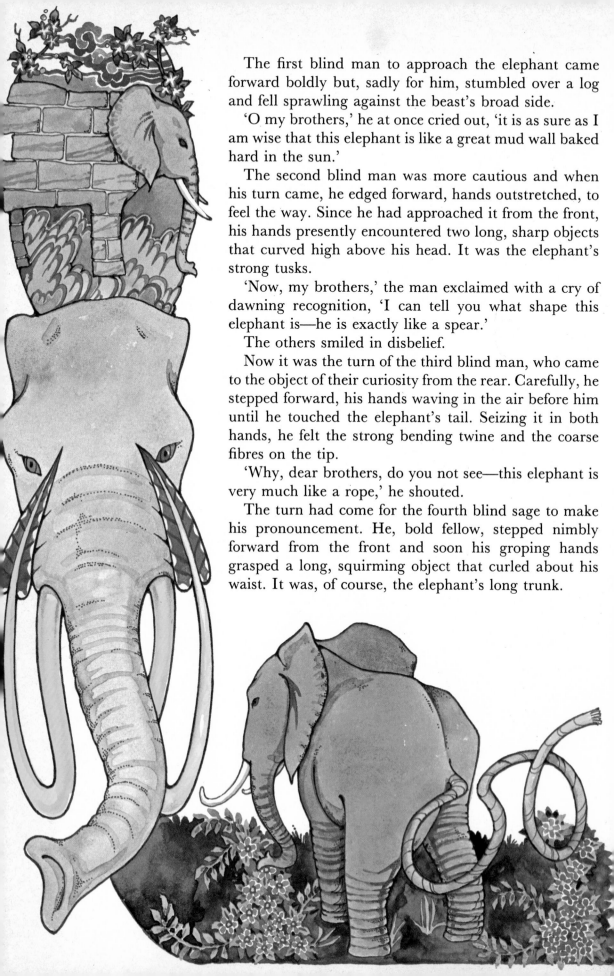

The first blind man to approach the elephant came forward boldly but, sadly for him, stumbled over a log and fell sprawling against the beast's broad side.

'O my brothers,' he at once cried out, 'it is as sure as I am wise that this elephant is like a great mud wall baked hard in the sun.'

The second blind man was more cautious and when his turn came, he edged forward, hands outstretched, to feel the way. Since he had approached it from the front, his hands presently encountered two long, sharp objects that curved high above his head. It was the elephant's strong tusks.

'Now, my brothers,' the man exclaimed with a cry of dawning recognition, 'I can tell you what shape this elephant is—he is exactly like a spear.'

The others smiled in disbelief.

Now it was the turn of the third blind man, who came to the object of their curiosity from the rear. Carefully, he stepped forward, his hands waving in the air before him until he touched the elephant's tail. Seizing it in both hands, he felt the strong bending twine and the coarse fibres on the tip.

'Why, dear brothers, do you not see—this elephant is very much like a rope,' he shouted.

The turn had come for the fourth blind sage to make his pronouncement. He, bold fellow, stepped nimbly forward from the front and soon his groping hands grasped a long, squirming object that curled about his waist. It was, of course, the elephant's long trunk.

'Ha, I thought as much,' he declared excitedly. 'This elephant much resembles a serpent.'

The others snorted their contempt.

The fifth, a tall old fellow with turban and white beard, chanced to touch the creature's ear.

'Good gracious, brothers,' he called out, 'even a blind man can see what shape the elephant resembles most. Why, he's mighty like a fan.'

That brought scoffing laughter from the remaining five.

At last, it was the turn of the sixth old fellow. He, bowed down with age, came forward slowly, passing beneath the elephant's trunk and tusks, so that his head came in contact with the beast's stout leg. Feeling it wonderingly with both hands, he called to the others in his wheezy, old voice.

'This sturdy pillar, brothers' mine, feels exactly like the trunk of the great areca palm tree.'

Of course, no one believed him.

Their curiosity satisfied, they all linked hands and followed their guide, Dookiram, back to the village. Once there, seated beneath a waving palm, the six blind men again began disputing loud and long. Each now had his own opinion, firmly based on his own experience, of what an elephant is really like. For after all, each had felt the elephant for himself and knew that *he* was right!

And so indeed he was. For depending on how the elephant is seen, each blind man was partly right, though all were in the wrong.

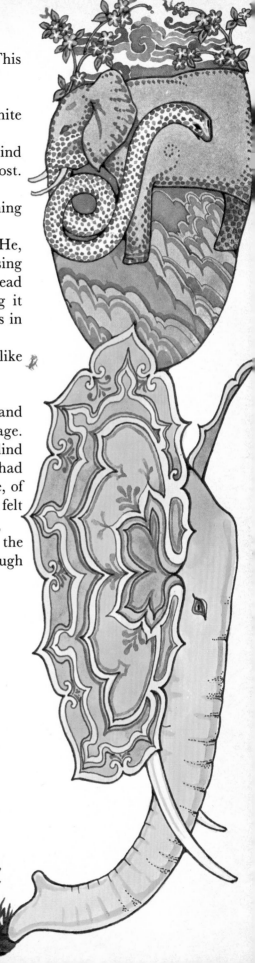

Beauty and the Beast

There once lived in France, a wealthy merchant who had three daughters, each more lovely than words can tell. He loved his daughters more than his entire fortune, and he loved his youngest daughter best of all because she was the kindest and most loving.

One day the good merchant made ready to leave on a trading voyage across the seas. Before departing, he called his daughters to him.

'Tell me,' he said, 'what presents shall I bring you?'

The first daughter curtseyed low before her father, and said, 'Bring me, I pray thee, Sire, a mirror of oriental crystal such that I may see reflected in it all the beauty under the sun.'

Next his second daughter curtseyed low and said, 'Bring me, I pray thee, Sire, a golden crown set with precious pearls, such that turns the dark of night into the light of day.'

Then the youngest daughter curtseyed low and said, 'Please bring me, Sire, a dark red rose.'

Then, because her father looked disappointed that she only wanted such a simple gift, she added, 'The best there is.'

The good merchant departed. He sailed into foreign ports, traded in their markets, sold his wares at thrice their value and bought others at three times less. He obtained a golden crown set with precious pearls that turned the dark of night into the light of day. And he purchased a crystal mirror that reflected all the beauty under the sun.

Yet nowhere could he find the special rose. 'How can I find what it is I know not?' thought he. 'Who is to say which rose is the best there is?'

In the gardens of kings and sultans he came upon many roses of great beauty. But no one could assure him that any one red rose was the best there was.

As he journeyed home disappointed, his ship was set upon by pirates and he barely escaped with his life, swimming alone to an uncharted island. He searched, but could find no members of his crew left alive.

He wandered up the shore and into a dense, dark forest. Not really knowing what he was doing, he pushed his way through the undergrowth. And the farther he went the easier it became. A beaten track appeared beneath his feet, the trees and bushes parted before him. From dawn to dusk he walked along the path which appeared beneath his feet, never hearing a beast roar, a snake hiss, an owl hoot or a bird sing. A deathly silence lay all about him.

But then, as night descended, he saw through the trees a glow which, as he drew near, he could see came from a magnificent palace, standing in a forest clearing. It shone with the light of blazing gold and precious gems. It hurt his eyes just to gaze upon it. All the palace windows were thrown open and from within came sweet music, such as the merchant had never before heard.

Entering the great courtyard through the open portals, he followed a path of white marble, past crystal fountains and fragrant blossoms of untold beauty and trees heavy with sweet, ripe fruits. He climbed a staircase carpeted with crimson velvet into the palace and ventured first into one chamber, then a second, a fifth and a tenth. Still there was not a soul to be seen. Everywhere his gaze met furnishings fit for a king: gold, silver, and ivory of elephant and mammoth.

61

The good merchant marvelled at such wealth, yet wondered even more at the absence of master and servants. And although there was no one to be seen the air was filled with soft melodious music.

After a while though, the merchant said to himself, 'This finery is all very well, but I wish there was something to eat.'

At once a table appeared before him, set with just a single place. Being very hungry, he ate his fill, drained three goblets of wine and then, feeling tired, made his way to a lofty bedchamber. He lay down upon a bed of swansdown, drew the silken canopy over him and instantly it grew dark as at twilight, and the music seemed to fade away.

Next morning, when he awoke, he looked out of the window and, to his great joy, perceived a grassy mound on which was growing a dark red rose of quite exquisite beauty. Its fragrance filled the air with sweet perfume.

Eagerly, he ran down to the palace gardens and plucked it from its bed.

At that same moment, with no black warning cloud, lightning flashed, thunder rolled and the earth shook beneath his feet. There appeared before him, as from the ground, a creature who was neither man nor beast, a monster most terrible to behold.

'I welcomed you as an honoured guest,' the beast roared in a savage voice. 'I gave you food and rest. Is this how you repay my kindness, by stealing my rose? Learn then your punishment: you must die this instant!'

On every side, a great chorus of savage voices took up the cry, 'You must die this instant!'

The good merchant shook with fear. On every side, from under every bush and tree, from the water and the ground, he beheld a host of evil spirits crawling towards him. He fell to his knees, crying that the rose was for his youngest, kindest daughter, not for himself.

The beast fell silent, then spoke again. 'I will pardon you on one condition. Within three days your daughter shall come here of her own accord, to suffer in your stead.'

With that he gave the merchant a golden ring and the poor man found himself transported home, still clutching the fateful rose. There amidst his family he related his adventure.

Straightaway the youngest daughter fell on her knees before him, crying, 'Gladly will I take your place, Sire. But mourn me not while yet I live. One day, God grant, I shall return to you.'

Three days soon passed and then, in silent sadness, she put the ring upon her finger and vanished with her rose. In no time at all she found herself within the palace gardens, standing before that grassy mound. And as she approached, the rose flew from her hands and settled in its former bed, blossoming more richly than before.

As she entered the palace, sweet music played on invisible strings and sumptuous food was served by unseen hands. As she sat down to dine she saw words of fire inscribe themselves upon the white marble wall:

'Welcome, Dear Beauty, have no fear
For you are Queen and Mistress here.'

Having eaten and found
no soul to thank, she made
her way to the lofty chamber and
slept soundly in the bed of swansdown.

Thus it was that the merchant's
lovely daughter came to live in the
enchanted palace. Each day, gorgeous robes
were laid before her. Each day, she was entertained
by new diversions. She would ride through the dark
forests in unharnessed carriages, the trees and bushes
parting before her. She would read and play music and
embroider as the fancy took her.

So time passed—the tale is sooner told than the deed is
done—and the merchant's youngest daughter grew
accustomed to her new life. Nothing made her fearful any
more. Daily she grew more fond of her gracious master,
though she had never seen him, for she saw that he loved
her more than he loved himself. He made her life as
happy and beautiful as he possibly could, and she longed
to hear his voice and to converse with him. The only way
he communicated with her was to write his messages in
words of fire upon the marble wall.

So she began to beseech him. But he would not listen
to her, afraid that his savage voice would destroy her
trust. She continued to beg him and, at last, unable to
resist her any longer, he wrote his final message on the
marble wall:

> 'In the garden at midday,
> Dear Beauty, you must say;
> Speak with me, my loyal servant.'

The merchant's lovely daughter could not conceal her
joy. Long before midday she was seated in the garden
and as the sun rose overhead, she said in a trembling
voice, 'Fear not, my kind and gracious master, that you

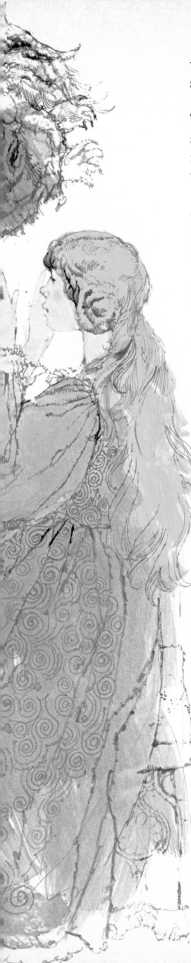

will scare me with your voice. Speak with me, my loyal
servant.'

From behind a nearby bush there came a piteous sigh.
Then a terrible voice rang out, wild and snarling. At first
she was filled with horror and not a little afraid but she
mastered her fear and as she listened to his words, so
wise and kind, her heart grew lighter.

From that time forth they conversed throughout the
day—the beauty and the beast. His snarling voice made
her afraid no longer and they would hold long conversa-
tions from dawn to dusk.

Time passed. But there came a day when the merchant's youngest daughter longed to see the beast with
her own eyes. Again she began to beg and beseech him.
For a long time he did not consent, afraid that she would
hate him once she set eyes on his repulsive form. Yet he
couldn't endure her tears and at last yielded to her pleas.

'I cannot go against your wishes, since I love you more
than I care for myself,' said the beast. 'I will grant your
wish, but I know it may destroy us both. Come to the
gardens in the shadows of the dusk and say—show
yourself to me, dear friend.'

Unalarmed and unafraid, she went directly to the
garden at the appointed hour and, as the sun was sinking
low, she called, 'Show yourself to me, dear friend.'

At a distance, the beast showed himself to her. But
fleetingly. He quickly moved across the path and disappeared into the bushes. At once she let out a cry of horror
and swooned upon the ground, so horrible indeed was
that awful creature.

When the maid regained her senses, she heard sobbing
as if a heart would break. She felt ashamed and sorry.
Mastering her timid heart, she spoke up firmly. 'Do not
weep, my friend, I fear your form no longer. Your ugly
shape is not your doing: true beauty lies within, not in
what is without.'

From that day forth, they walked and talked together
in trust and wisdom; and the merchant's daughter slowly
lost her fear. All day they were together. At breakfast and
dinner they ate their fill of sweetmeats and refreshed
themselves with meads and sherbets. Of a morning and
afternoon, they would wander through the verdant
gardens or drive in the dark forests in a carriage which
needed no horses.

One night, however, the merchant's lovely daughter dreamed that her father was lying ill, and an inconsolable grief fell upon her. When she told the beast of her deep sorrow, he, kind soul, at once despatched her home.

'Go forthwith,' he said, 'but heed this, dear Beauty, should you not return within three days I shall die that very instant, because I love you dearly and cannot live without you.'

He put the golden ring upon her finger and straightaway she found herself transported home. How happy her father and her sisters were; how astonished they were to hear her story; and how swiftly the good merchant recovered his sound health.

But when the hour drew near for her return, her sisters begged her not to go. 'Let him perish, as he deserves,' they said.

'Should I repay such kindness with a selfish act,' the girl replied, 'I would not be worthy of life upon this earth.'

But her sisters, being envious of her devotion, played a trick upon her. Secretly, they put back by one full hour all the household clocks.

Thus when the final hour came, the merchant's youngest daughter felt a piercing heartache and looked constantly at her father's clocks. At last her heart could bear the pain no longer and, one minute before the appointed time, she put the golden ring upon her finger and found herself once more before the splendid palace.

All was still. No music played, no birdsong echoed from the verdant gardens, and no answer met her when she called. With fast-beating heart, she ran to the grassy mound and there beheld the beast lying on the ground, clasping the rose in his misshapen paw. Gently she tried to rouse him, thinking that he'd fallen asleep while waiting for her. But she found no life in his body.

Her eyes brimmed with shame and pity. She put her slender arms about his ugly neck and kissed him tenderly, a single tear falling on his death-cold head.

No sooner had she kissed him than lightning flashed on every side and thunder struck the grassy mound. The girl fell senseless to the ground.

When she awoke she found herself in a chamber of white marble, sitting on a golden throne beside a young and handsome prince. Before them stood her dear father and her sisters amidst a host of resplendent courtiers.

The handsome prince spoke thus to her: 'When I was but an infant, an evil sorceress, being angry with the king, my father, turned me into that beast whom you befriended. Full thirty years I suffered thus, enticing eleven maidens to my enchanted palace. You were the twelfth. But only you could break the spell because you grew to love me truly, forgetting my form and seeing the kindness in my heart and the wisdom in my mind. I beg you now to be my queen.'

Without more ado a grand wedding was held amid great rejoicing. And their happiness, being built on goodness, was complete.

Five Monstrous Creatures

An old German farmer had in his yard an ox, a ram, a goose, a cock and a pig. As guests were coming to dinner on the Sabbath, he told his wife, 'Old woman, we need meat for the Sabbath so I am going to kill the cock tomorrow morning.'

Overhearing this unpleasant news, the cock scurried off to the forest as fast as his legs would carry him.

When the farmer went to wring his neck before sunrise, the cock was nowhere to be seen.

That same evening, the farmer told his wife, 'I could not find the cock, so I shall have to kill the pig instead.'

Overhearing this, the pig, too, fled for dear life to the safety of the forest.

The old man searched high and low for the pig, but without success.

'How strange,' he said. 'First the cock and now the pig. I shall have to slaughter the ram.'

When the ram heard this bad news, he went to the goose and suggested they should run away together—or they would surely both end up in the pot. So, as soon as it was dark, the ram and the goose made off to the forest.

Though the farmer searched every nook and cranny of the yard he could find no trace of the ram or the goose.

'That leaves only the ox,' he sighed. 'A pity to kill him,

but we must have meat for the holy day.'

On hearing these ill tidings, the ox plodded off to join his comrades in the forest.

Throughout the summer, life was happy and food was plentiful. The runaway creatures had not a care in the world. But summer passed all too quickly and winter was soon not far off. When the autumn leaves began to wither and thin layers of ice covered the water holes, the ox approached the other animals.

'Listen to me, brothers,' he said. 'Winter will soon be upon us. We must build ourselves a hut to shelter in.'

The ram, however, answered, 'I have a warm woollen coat and I shall winter in that.'

The pig said, 'No hard frosts bother me. I'll burrow a hole in the ground with my snout and do without a hut.'

The goose also refused to join the ox, saying, 'I shall use one wing as a pillow, bury my head in it, and use the other as an eiderdown. The icy winds will not worry me.'

The cock, too, shook his head and said, 'I shall shelter

from the winter in a fir tree.'

The ox saw that he could expect no help from his fellow creatures. He would have to do all the building himself.

'As you wish,' he sighed, 'but I shall build a wooden hut for myself.'

So he built himself a strong wooden hut, stoked up the stove and settled down beside it, snug and warm.

Almost overnight autumn gave way to winter, the first snows came and the wind sent icy blasts through the trees. The ram rushed hither and thither, but despite his woollen fleece, he shivered and shook and could not keep warm. At last he went to the ox.

'Baa-baa-baa, baa-baa-baa! Let me into your hut,' he said.

'Certainly not,' replied the ox. 'I asked you to help me build the hut, and you said you had a warm coat and did not need my hut.'

'If you don't let me in,' cried the ram, 'I'll break down your door with my strong horns.'

That worried the ox.

'Perhaps I'd better let him in,' he mumbled, 'or I shall have no door. All right, Brother Ram, come on in.'

The ram entered the warm hut and settled on a bench beside the stove.

Not long afterwards the pig arrived.

'Grunt, grunt, grunt. Let me in to warm myself,' he shouted.

'Certainly not,' said the ox. 'I asked for your help, but you said the frosts did not worry you and that you would burrow a hole and keep yourself warm.'

'If you don't let me in,' warned the pig, 'I'll knock down your door-posts with my strong snout.'

That worried the ox, and finally he decided to let in the pig. In hobbled the pig and wandered downstairs to the cellar.

After the pig came the goose.

'Hiss, hiss, hiss! Ox, let me in to get warm,' he cried.

'No, Brother Goose, you cannot come in,' said the ox. 'You have two warm wings remember—one for a pillow, the other for an eiderdown. You said you would not be cold.'

'If you don't open the door,' warned the goose, 'I shall peck all the moss from your window.'

70

The ox had to give in. So the goose waddled in and perched on a post by the door.

A little later the cock arrived.

'Cock-a-doodle-do, cock-a-doodle-do!' he crowed. 'Ox, let me into your warm hut. I'm freezing out here.'

'No, I shall not, Brother Cock,' replied the ox. 'Go and winter in a fir tree, as you said you would.'

'If you don't let me in,' said the cock, 'I shall fly on to your roof and peck holes in it to let the icy draughts through.'

Of course the ox had to open the door, and in strutted the cock. He flew up to a beam above the door and settled down to sleep.

So the five creatures lived together in the warm hut. But their peace was shortlived, for a big grey wolf and a huge brown bear came to hear of the new residents.

'Let's go to the hut, eat them all and live there ourselves,' the bear suggested to the wolf.

On that they at once agreed. But they argued about who should enter the hut first.

'You go first,' said the wolf. 'You are the stronger.'

'No, you go,' replied the bear. 'I am too clumsy. You're nimbler than me.'

At last the wolf gave in and burst open the door of the hut in the middle of the night, while the five friends were sleeping. But no sooner had he passed through the doorway than the ox pinned him to the wall with his long horns and the ram butted him from the side.

From the cellar the pig grunted loudly, 'I'm sharpening the axe. I'm sharpening the knife. I'll skin that wolf alive, I will.'

From his other side, the goose pecked the wolf as hard as he was able. Meanwhile, the cock hopped about on the beam above the door, screeching, 'That's the way, give it to him! I'll slit his throat and hang him from the beam.'

Outside the hut, the bear could hear this great hullabaloo and took to his heels, rushing pell-mell into the trees. In the meantime, the wolf twisted this way and that, his grey fur flying, his ribs battered and bruised. At long last he tore himself free and dashed for dear life after the bear.

When the two animals had left the hut far behind they fell in a heap exhausted, and the wolf told his story.

'Oh, brown bear, it was terrible, just terrible! Those ruffians all but skinned me alive. First a huge fellow in a

black smock charged at me, knocking me against the wall, and then set upon me with two great clubs. Then another rogue, a shorter grey-cloaked fellow, butted me from one side, while his mate, all in white, scratched me from the other side. All the while, the smallest of this band of robbers, wearing a red apron, pranced about on a beam above my head screaming, "That's the way, give it to him! I'll slit his throat and hang him from the beam." Then, from the cellar, another brigand bellowed, "I'm sharpening the axe. I'm sharpening the knife. I'll skin that wolf alive, I will!" I was lucky to escape with my life, I can tell you.'

From that day on, the wolf and the bear kept well clear of the hut, fearing the five monstrous creatures who dwelt within. So the ox, the ram, the goose, the cock and the pig lived together with no one to disturb their peace.

Ngarri Jandu and the Nimmamoo

In Yamminga times, when the spirit snake Bannin-booroo, the eaglehawk Warragunna and the kangaroo Yonggar roamed the bushlands of Australia, the people had much fear of the Ngarri, the devil spirits that lurked in the bush. Ngarri spirits were dazzling white like the sun and it hurt the eyes just to catch sight of them. Sometimes they took the shape of a giant woman who rushed through the bush shrieking and yelling, as a wife does when she's angry. Other times they took the shape of a giant man who stomped about the earth roaring 'kallee-gooroo,' like a bull.

One day in the far-off times, two young nimmamoo boys went out into the bush to look for the sweet geerbaju honey. One boy carried a blackwood bowl, while the other took a thorn. It was not long before they saw bees gathering nectar in a grove of blossoming trees. As the bees flew off, the two nimmamoo boys tried to follow their flight so that they could find their store of honey. But the bees were so small that it was hard to see which way they went.

All the same, one of the boys managed to catch a bee in his two hands, as it was busy taking nectar from a flower. Carefully, he held it up between a finger and his thumb, the mother of his hand. Then, pricking his bare arm with the thorn, he squeezed out a drop of blood with which to stick a tiny white feather to the bee's back.

Now the nimmamoo boys could follow the bee in flight and it took them right to where the sweet geerbaju honey was stored. Since the bee had disappeared into the hollow of a tree trunk, the boys quickly shinned up the tree to get at the honey. The higher they climbed, the more loudly they could hear the busy humming, humming of the bees inside the trunk. Soon they reached the nest and took as much honey as they wished, filling a

74

quarter of their wooden bowl.

Using the very same trick with the white feather, they discovered several stores of honey that day and by sundown their blackwood bowl was almost full. They decided they would climb one last tree before going back to camp. However, while they were both in the topmost branches of the tree, a Ngarri Jandu spirit man crept up to the tree. He had smelled out the two nimmamoo boys and tracked them down.

So when they climbed down, the spirit man snatched them up and carried them off in a big wicker basket. Though they hollered loud and long, it did no good: they were trapped and in the clutches of Ngarri Jandu. Before long they came to his home in the hollow of a juniper tree and he took each boy out of his basket and pushed him inside the tree, covering the opening with a thick rind of bark.

The two nimmamoo boys were very frightened, for they now found themselves amongst a squirming nest of Ngarri babba or spirit boys who had once been nimmamoo like themselves. They had all been carried off by the Ngarri Jandu and turned into Ngarri babba. The spirit man kept the Ngarri babba to eat.

With the two nimmamoo boys safe inside his den, the Ngarri Jandu man went off to hunt for food to feed his spirit boys. He caught the langoor possum, the woggal snake, the yoongga lizard, and brought all his wallee meat back to the tree for the spirit boys and the two nimmamoo. He wanted to make them all fat enough to eat. Each day he went out hunting, and each day he brought back more snakes, possums and lizards to eat. And each day he himself ate the fattest of the Ngarri babba. However much they screamed and kicked he picked them up, popped them in his mouth and swallowed them whole, bones and all.

The two nimmamoo boys became even more frightened. They knew that their turn was coming soon and they would be turned into Ngarri babba; then they would be eaten. They had to escape before it was too late.

One morning, when the spirit man was out hunting, one of the nimmamoo boys pulled the nose-bone from his nose and, it being hollow, blew through it as hard as he could on to the bark door. He blew and blew until his

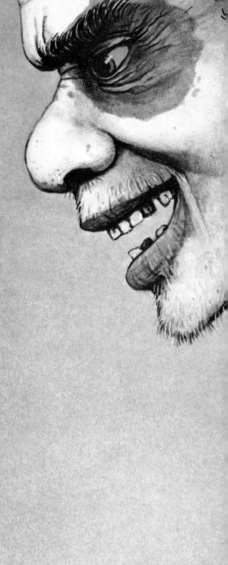

75

cheeks swelled up like a toad's. Yet he could not shift the bark door.

Then the second nimmamoo boy took out his nose-bone and blew through it. He was stronger than his companion and, suddenly, the bark door fell away. At once the two boys jumped out of the hollow tree and ran as fast as their legs would carry them towards their camp.

Meanwhile the Ngarri Jandu was hunting wallee meat and looking for more young boys to carry off to his tree. It was not until late evening that he reached home to find the boys gone. He flew into a terrible rage. Seeking their footprints in the dust and their smell on the wind, he rushed off in pursuit.

By this time the boys had travelled a long way but they were still some distance from their camp. Luckily for them, however, they came across a band of hunters in the bush.

'Ngarri Jandu is after us,' they cried. 'Please kill him with your spears so that he won't catch us.'

'Ngow-ai,' the hunters solemnly replied. 'It shall be done.'

When the Ngarri Jandu came in sight, the hunters kept their promise and rushed at him with their spears. They hurled spear after spear at him, then beat him with their clubs. But the spears did not pierce his body because his body was as hard as stone. And the clubs did not break his bones because his bones were as tough as flint. Although the hunters fought him 'til sundown, they were unable to stop him. At last, weak and tired, they put aside their weapons and let him pass.

So the Ngarri Jandu continued in pursuit of the two nimmamoo boys. At each camp he came to, the men attacked him with their sharp spears and stout clubs. Yet they could not harm him. He passed by unhurt.

Finally he came to the camp where the boys lived and was about to snatch them up when an old man flung a spear at him which had mirooroo magic in it. The spear whistled through the air and caught the spirit man on the heel of his left foot—where his heart was. He crashed to the ground, writhing like a stricken snake. Soon he was dead.

Yool-burroo-boora. All these things took place a long time ago.

Jack O'Lantern

There was once a tinker of Ballingarry, down in County Limerick in Ireland. As you are bound to know, all tinkers are as poor as field mice. So it was with Jack the tinker. Though, 'tis true, he was not as poor as he was humble, for he had a cottage to himself without a landlord, and a small garden behind with a fine apple tree therein. For a good part of the year Jack travelled the country, leaving his wife to mind the cottage and the garden.

One day while on his travels, Jack encountered a wayfarer and hailed him politely.

The wayfarer took a liking to the happy tinker and said to him, 'I can grant you three wishes. Do the best you can with them, for such a chance will never come your way again.'

Jack set to thinking hard and said, 'Now that you mention it, for sure I've an old armchair back home. Every visitor I have sits down in that armchair and makes me stand. So I wish that whoever sits in that chair shall stick there till I give the word.'

'Granted,' said the stranger. 'Now let's hear your

second wish, and I'd have you know to ask for something useful this time.'

Jack fell to thinking once again, then said, 'I've a tree in my garden that bears fine apples. But all the scalliwags for miles around steal every apple off that tree. So I wish that whoever goes to steal an apple will stick to that tree until I give the word.'

'Granted,' said the stranger. 'Now, listen well, this is your last chance. Think of something really useful and say your piece.'

Jack thought and thought, then smiled and said, 'I know. My wife has a leather woolbag in which she keeps all her scraps of wool, and odds and ends besides. But little hooligans come to my house and tip all the wool upon the floor. I wish everything in that bag would stay there till I give the word.'

'Granted,' said the man. 'But, my dear fellow, you've done not a scrap of good by yourself.'

With that he went on his way shaking his head, while Jack the tinker turned for home as poor and carefree as before.

Some time after Jack's return, he slipped and fell and broke his leg, so he had to lie at home in bed the whole year through, unable to earn a living. His poor family were near starvation's door when a stranger chanced to pass by their cottage and entered unannounced.

'I observe,' the stranger said to Jack, 'that your family's in great need. You are all starving, that's clear enough. Now I'm willing to strike a bargain with you: come to me at the end of seven years and I'll see you live in comfort until then.'

'But who are you?' Jack enquired.

'Who am I?' echoed the stranger. 'I'll tell you straight enough—I'm the Devil!'

'What matter?' murmured Jack, looking at his starving children. 'I'll take your offer soon enough.' And Jack gave his word to be ready at the end of seven years.

The Devil went on his way, leaving Jack as prosperous as a tinker ever has been. Henceforth there was never any lack of food within the house. No more did Jack go a'tinkering from place to place, or even if he did, it was more for pleasure's sake. Nor did his wife need to go a'woolpicking for her neighbours; she stayed at home, and all went well for the tinker and his wife, to the amazement of all the folks from round about.

In no time at all, the Devil went clean out of Jack's busy mind. Seven years passed by in bliss and comfort, but when the last day of the last year came round, Jack had a visitor.

'Your seven years are up,' the Devil said. 'I've kept my side of the bargain, now you keep yours.'

'Sure enough,' said Jack. 'It's off I'll be with you in just a jiffy. Give me a moment to say farewell to my dear wife. In the meantime, just you sit here in my armchair and wait for me. I'll not be long.'

The Devil sat himself down in Jack's armchair and waited. Since Jack had known his wife for going on twenty years, it didn't take him long to say goodbye. So he was soon back before the Devil.

'Come on,' he said, 'let's be going.'

The Devil made to rise but, pull and jerk as he might, he could not budge from out the chair. He let out a string of curses that were heard across three townlands, and struggled fiercely. But it was no use. Seeing that he was stuck fast, he appealed to Jack.

'I'll grant you another seven years and twice as many riches if you will let me go.'

'That's fair enough,' said Jack. 'Up and be away with you—back to where you belong.'

The Devil was gone like a flash of lightning. Now Jack the tinker was doubly wealthy and his family lived in peace and comfort. But the seven years seemed to go twice as fast as before, for now Jack had twice as much to spend. Soon his time was up again and the Devil was at his door.

'I'll have none of your shenanigans this time, my lad,' said the Devil. 'Come on, let's go straightaway.'

Jack made ready quickly, but said, as he left the house, 'Let's make our way through my garden. Since I won't see it again, I'd like a last look at my apple tree.'

The Devil consented, and they walked together to the bottom of the garden and stood beneath the apple tree, now overloaded with juicy apples.

'The day is warm,' said Jack, 'shall we not take some apples with us to eat on the way? You are taller than I am—be so good as to pick us a couple of big'uns.'

'I will do that same,' the Devil said. And springing up he caught a large red apple, yet could not pull it off, nor let go of it. He stuck there swinging to and fro. He tugged and pulled, but it was no use.

Letting fly a curse that this time was heard from Galway down to Killarney, he shouted at Jack, 'I'll grant you another seven years and thrice the wealth you had at first. Just let me down from out this tree.'

Jack freed the Devil and off he raced without delay.

Now Jack and his family lived in wealth and plenty for seven more years. But just as autumn follows summer,

81

and bad luck good, so at last the time was up and the Devil stood once more before him.

'To be sure now I'll stand none of your hanky-panky. And when I get you down in hell I'll make you pay for what you've done to me,' he said to Jack.

Jack bid farewell to his wife, took down the leather woolbag from the wall and went off with the Devil.

They walked some way in silence, and then Jack said, 'Do you know I had some fun when I was still a lad. I used to jump in and out of this old woolbag. Mind you, I was quick and nimble then.'

'Any fool could do that,' said the Devil with a grin.

'Go on, I bet you couldn't do it,' retorted Jack. 'You're too big and clumsy.'

Jack held the woolbag open, and the Devil sprang right in. In an instant the bag was shut with the Devil firmly trapped inside. How that Devil howled and screamed! But Jack would not listen. He marched over the hills with his bag on one shoulder until he came to a cornfield. There he saw three strong men threshing grain with wooden flails.

'Hey, boyoes,' shouted Jack. 'I've a bag here that's stiff and heavy. Will you give it a thrashing for me, to limber it up like?'

The men gladly walloped the bag, but so heavy was it that it broke their flails.

'Be off with you and that bag of yours,' they cried. 'The Devil himself must be in it.'

'Oh, maybe it's himself that's in it, right enough,' said Jack with a chuckle.

He walked on with the bag over his shoulder until he came to a water mill.

Going up to the miller, he said, 'I want to soften this bag a little. Will you let it go through your mill?'

The man agreed and Jack threw his bag into the mill. The miller was a mite surprised to hear a cracking and a smashing coming from the bag. He was even more astonished, and not a little cross, when his mill broke down.

'Get away with you,' he shouted. 'What's that you've got in your bag, the Devil begorrah?'

'Sure and maybe it's the truth you're telling,' said Jack, picking up his bag and walking off with it.

Presently, Jack came to a blacksmith's forge where six

sturdy men were hammering at a piece of iron.

'Top of the morning to you, boys,' called Jack. 'What do you say to giving this old bag of mine a few hard whacks? It's that stiff and weighty!'

'Why now should we not?' said they.

The six men took their hammers and laid about the bag. With each blow it flew up in the air; this so enraged the men that they hammered even harder until they were tired and panting.

'Phew, the Devil himself must be in that bag,' they railed at Jack.

One strong smith then lost his temper, seized a red hot iron from the fire and thrust it through the bag, catching the Devil unawares, so that he could not sit down for a whole year afterwards!

The Devil howled and screamed, 'Let me out. Let me out. I'll leave you in peace for good and give you riches four times over. Just leave me be.'

At last Jack opened up the woolbag and let the Devil out. Away he shot as fast as his battered legs would carry him. Jack went back home and lived in plenty with his

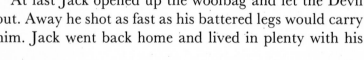

family for many a long year. But when he was very, very
old, he felt just about ready to make his weary way to the
other world. So off he went and stood before the gates of
the good place. He knocked politely.

'Go away,' came a voice. 'Go back to the one you have
worked for all your life. You can't come in here.'

So Jack the tinker went and knocked on the gates of
the bad place.

'Who's there?' came a voice.

'Jack the tinker from Ballingarry,' Jack said.

'Don't let him in!' screamed a frightened voice. 'He
beat me black and blue and scorched my seat so badly I
couldn't sit down for a month of Sundays!'

They would not let him in the bad place so back Jack
went to the other place. They would not let him into
heaven, so Jack was condemned to travel the world,
always in the dark, and carrying only a small lantern.

He was to have no rest, but wander over bogs,
swamps, moors and lonely places, leading folk astray. So
Jack the tinker roams still, forever travelling the road
until the Day of Judgement.

Folk know him now as Jack O'Lantern.

The Children of Sky and Earth

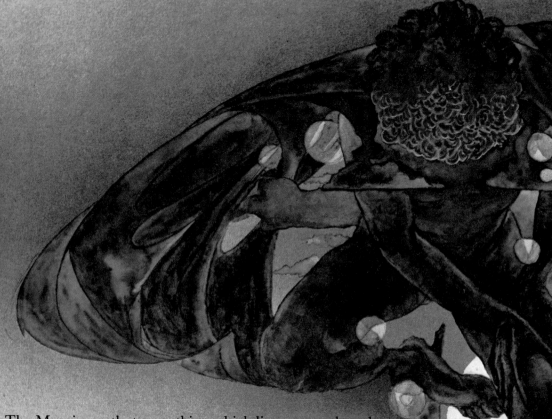

The Maoris say that everything which lives on earth and in the sky is descended from Papa the boundless sky above us, and Rangi the earth that lies below us. In the beginning Papa and Rangi were not yet divided, and lay clinging to each other. That is why there was no daylight on earth or in the sky.

Thus it was for one part of time, and for another, and for ten parts, and a hundred, and a thousand. These parts of time made up the long, dark nights, which were called Po. As long as Po lasted, there was no light, there was only darkness.

Meanwhile, the children of Papa and Rangi grew up without ever knowing daylight, and they grew weary of

86

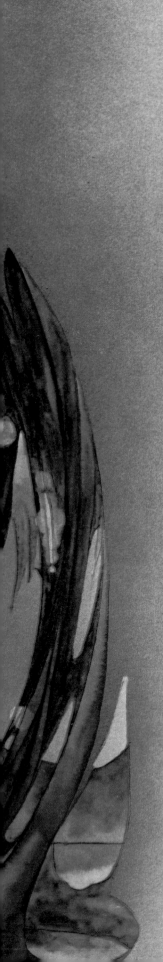

their eternal gloom. Finally, the children of the sky and the earth set to wondering what to do.

'Let us decide what we shall do about Papa and Rangi,' they said. 'For it is they who deny us light.'

Then it was that Tu Matawenga, the fiercest and most warlike of the children of Papa and Rangi, spoke up.

'Let us slay Papa and Rangi so that we may have light,' he said.

'No,' said Tanay Mahoot, god and father of the forests. 'It is better to separate them. Let us make the sky rise high above us and the earth sink down beneath our feet. Let Papa Sky be far distant and let Rangi Earth stay close by us, as our provident mother.'

All the brothers agreed with Tanay Mahoot except Tafiri Ma Teya, god and father of storms. He did not wish Papa and Rangi to be separated for he liked the dark. But the decision was taken in spite of him.

Then up stood Rongo Ma Tanay, god and father of all crops. He tried with all his might to tear the sky and the earth apart, but he could not do it.

Next to try was Tangaroa, god and father of the oceans and all that lives in the water, yet he too was unable to part Rangi from Papa.

He was followed by Tikitiki, god and father of wild berries. He too failed to part Papa and Rangi.

Next came Tu Matawenga, the fiercest of the gods, and father of all warring peoples, but even he was unsuccessful.

When all the other brothers had failed, Tanay Mahoot, god and father of the forests, slowly got to his feet. First he tried to tear sky from earth with his bare hands but to no avail. Then, with his feet planted firmly on earth and his broad shoulders braced against the sky, he made a mighty effort and tore Rangi from Papa.

The sky and the earth groaned and wept in their great grief. 'Why do you punish us, your parents?' they cried. 'To part us is just as cruel as killing us.'

Tanay Mahoot did not answer. Deeper and deeper he pressed the earth beneath him, higher and higher he raised the sky. And as the two moved farther apart, the darkness receded and it grew light.

In the clear light of day could be seen a whole host of people born to Rangi and Papa, and who until then had lain hidden between their bodies.

Now it was that Tafiri Ma Teya, god and father of storms, who had not wanted Rangi and Papa to be parted, decided to take revenge and wage war on all his brothers. He hated all that was bright and beautiful. So he followed Papa and made his home in the boundless sky, taking counsel with him concerning his revenge.

Together, Papa and Tafiri whipped up a mighty storm of winds which were despatched to all four corners of the earth: one to the west, one to the south, one to the east, and one to the north. They were quickly followed by raging squalls, whirlwinds, storm clouds, rain clouds, dark and gloomy clouds and fire clouds—heralds of the hurricane, and of thunder and lightning. And in the thick of them all rushed Tafiri the avenger.

Tanay Mahoot and his tall forests were standing proud and unsuspecting when these storms struck and the fiery breath of Tafiri's lightning scorched them. Huge trees came crashing down, bark and branches broke off and flew in all directions. In no time at all the earth was littered with fallen trees, broken boughs and branches, all left as decaying fodder for the worms and ants.

Having taken his revenge on Tanay Mahoot and his forests, Tafiri next turned towards the sea and let loose his fury on his brother Tangaroa, god of the oceans and father of all the denizens of the deep. Huge waves rolled angrily across the sea, water spouts and whirlpools circled round. Tangaroa took fright and dived down into the depths, leaving two of his children to fend for themselves.

These two sons of Tangaroa were Ica Teray, father of fish, and Tu Tay Veciveci, father of reptiles. They now began to quarrel.

'Let us hide in the sea,' cried Ica Teray.

'Let us hide on dry land,' said Tu Tay Veciveci.

They argued for quite a while until, at last, Ica Teray warned his brother, 'On dry land you and your kin will be caught and killed. Before being cooked, your scales will be scraped off with dried ferns.'

In reply Veciveci said, 'Beware yourself if you remain in the sea. For when guests come to dinner they will be given a dish of vegetables with you served up on top, seasoned and roasted.'

So they parted. The fish took shelter in the ocean depths and the reptiles slithered on to dry land and concealed themselves in the shrubs and trees. The god of the oceans, Tangaroa, was furious at half his family deserting him and sheltering with the forest god Tanay Mahoot. From then on, he vowed, he would not be kind to the children of the forest. And because of his anger at the loss of half his children, Tangaroa overturns boats in strong gales, uproots trees, sweeps up houses and sends his greedy waves crashing along the shores. He engulfs all insects, birds and even mighty trees that creep too close to his waters, and he carries them off into his boundless depths.

In the meantime, Tafiri Ma Teya, father of storms, fell upon his brothers Rongo Ma Tanay, god and father of crops, and Tikitiki, god and father of wild berries. But Rangi Mother Earth protected the one and the other, so as to save them for mankind. So well did she hide Rongo and Tikitiki in the earth, that the god of storms could not find them.

Finally Tafiri threw himself upon his land brother, Tu Matawenga. He flew at him in all his fury, but Tu Matawenga, father of all warring people, was unafraid. All his brothers had given way before Tafiri: Tanay and his kin had been conquered; Tangaroa and his children had hidden in land and sea; Rongo Ma Tanay and Tikitiki had sheltered in the earth. Only Tu Matawenga, the man creature, stood unflinching on the breast of Mother Earth. He displayed much courage and cunning in battle and, as the fury of the god of storms abated, Tu Matawenga remained unconquered.

When he had warded off the onslaught of the storms, Tu Matawenga set to thinking: his brothers had all deserted him in his lone battle with Tafiri. Why should he not now teach them a lesson for being so cowardly? First he turned to deal with Tanay Mahoot. Gathering a bundle of leaves from the fanaka tree, he wound them into loops and left these snares about the forest. The children of Tanay were often trapped and now none of them can run or fly freely about the forest for fear of being caught by men.

Next Tu Matawenga took revenge on his brother Tangaroa. From harakeki flax, he braided a net and cast it deep into the sea to drag Tangaroa's children on to the dry land.

Then he sought out his brothers Rongo Ma Tanay and Tikitiki. He recognised them by their leaves and berries, and he made a wooden digging stick, wove a wicker basket and dug up his brothers, throwing them into his basket.

Thus it was Tu Matawenga dealt with all his brothers for not coming to his aid when he alone battled with Tafiri, the god of storms. Tu Matawenga made his brothers his food and drink. Only the god of the storms, Tafiri Ma Teya, remained invincible and unavailable as food. He has remained the enemy of man creature forever. Even now he still tries to defeat his man brother with storms and hurricanes.

Because of Tafiri's savage fury at the parting of Papa and Rangi, the greater part of the land disappeared during his war against his brothers. It was flooded by Tafiri's kith and kin: the winter storms, the snow blizzards, the rain torrents and the unrelenting hailstones. Altogether they flooded so much land that nowadays only a small part of it rises above the waters.

Since the time when Rangi was torn apart from Papa, it has become light above the earth; and the many children of Rangi and Papa who had been concealed in the folds of their bodies have emerged into the light and given forth fruit of their own. These first living beings were very like the people of today; it is their descendants who roam the earth.

Although, the boundless sky remains separated from his wife, the earth, their abiding love lives on. Gentle sighs fly up to the sky from the earthly breast, rising above the wooded hills and green valleys. Men creatures call these sighs the mists. In his turn, the sky grieves for his beloved Rangi in long nights of gloom, dropping tears upon her breast. Man creatures call these tears the dewdrops.

The Fern Girl

Old woman Baiberikeen, mistress of five cows, went about her work, and lived off the milk of her five cows. Then, one night, the five cows suddenly disappeared from sight—each and every one. For four days together the old woman sought her cows all over Mongolia, but to no avail. On the fifth day, as she made her way towards the east, she came upon Mistress Crow sitting in a tree.

'I have lost my five cows,' she told the crow. 'And now I am on my way to find them. May it be that you, Mistress Crow, have seen them?'

'Carrrhh, carrrhh. If I had, I should not tell you,' replied Mistress Crow. 'You drove me away when I was picking at the chaff in your barn, you threw a stick at me and hurt my back. I shall not tell you. Carrrhh, carrrhh.'

On went the old woman and presently encountered Master Crow.

'Master Crow,' she began, 'I have lost my cows and have wandered the land looking for them. The skin is almost rubbed from my feet, that far have I come. You have keen eyes and ears; surely you know where my cows are? Pray tell me and I shall reward you well.'

'Chulup, chalip. No, even should I know, I should not tell,' answered Master Crow. 'When I was once pecking at a cow pat you chased me away, hurled a piece of dried cow dung at me and all but crushed me. I shall not tell you. Chulup, chalip.'

Old Baiberikeen went on her way. She had not gone
far when she met Master Eagle, perched proudly on top
of a tree.

'Master Eagle,' she began, 'I have lost five cows,
walked many, many miles, rubbed all the skin from my
feet, but have still not found them. Surely you know
where my cows are?'

'I know right enough,' said Master Eagle. 'Go east-
wards from here and you will come to a clearing. On the
sunny side is a pretty hillock on which stands a tree with
roots deep down in the soil and branches reaching low to
the ground. Under that tree are your five cows with five
new-born calves. Go there and you will find them.'

On hearing this, old Mistress Baiberikeen cheered up
at once and stepped out boldly. In no time at all she
arrived at the clearing and found her cows at the foot of
the great tree. And with them were five sturdy calves.

Yet as she tethered each calf to its mother and got
ready to drive them home, she spotted beneath the tree a
most uncommon fern with lacelike leaves of many
colours.

'I fancy I shall pull up that fern, take it home and
make it my child,' the old woman murmured.

Thereupon she dug up the fern without harm to roots
or leaves, placed it gently under her arm and set off with
her cows.

Back home, she carefully wrapped the fern in a blanket
and went out to the meadow to milk her cows.

When she had finished milking two of the five cows she
heard from her yurta a faint jingle like the sound made
by a falling thimble. She jumped up; in her haste to get
indoors she overturned the milk pail and spilled all the
milk. But she was so excited that she didn't bother about
the milk. She rushed towards the yurta. On entering her
home, she quickly unwrapped the blanket and gazed

upon the fern. But plainly the fern was still a fern and nothing more.

'Eeee-eee,' she cried in her disappointment, 'I should not have been so hasty, upsetting the milk like that.' And she returned to her milking.

When she had done with a third cow, she heard a jingle, like that made by a needle falling, in her yurta. She again tipped over the milk as she rushed to the yurta and looked eagerly inside the blanket. But plainly the fern was still a fern.

'What was that noise then?' she wondered as she returned to her cows. When she had finished milking a fourth cow, she heard a jingle like that of scissors falling in her yurta. Springing up at once she tripped over the pail of milk and ran towards her home. But there was nothing: the fern was still a fern.

Yet then, as she completed her milking, a baby's cry was heard from inside the yurta. Knocking over her pail as she rushed towards the sound, she entered her yurta, pulled back the blanket and there lay the most lovely baby girl dressed in a little lacelike dress of many colours.

Old Baiberikeen was overjoyed. She took the baby in her arms, kissed it all over, ran to the meadow where she squeezed a last drop of milk from her cows and fed it to the child.

Thus they lived as the days grew into months and the months into years. As the maid grew up, so her lovely lace dress grew with her. Soon she was a beautiful young girl with blue-grey eyes like chalcedony, pale lips like chiselled marble, a fair face like the petals of a flower and dark brows like two black sables. Through her dress showed her body, through her body her bones, and through her bones her brain quivering like quicksilver.

One day the son of Hara Haan, a close neighbour of old woman Baiberikeen, happened to pass the yurta. He was playing a game with some sticks: tossing them high into the air, he tried to catch them before they fell to the ground. One stick landed right in the chimney of the old woman's yurta.

'Baiberikeen,' the young man cried, 'throw back my stick please.'

'Take his stick, my child,' whispered old Baiberikeen to her daughter. 'Go and give it to the young man.'

Opening the door flap shyly, the maid threw the stick outside. When Hara Haan's son saw her he thought she was the loveliest creature he had ever set eyes on. He fell deeply in love with her at once.

Entering the yurta, the young man spoke to old Baiberikeen of his love for her daughter.

'Certainly you may take her as your wife,' the old woman said. 'My bride price is a pair of well-fed oxen and two young mares. Bring them here and you shall have her for your wife.'

The young man hurried home, and came riding back driving a pair of well-fed oxen, two young mares, and a horse for his bride. And he received his reward. Taking the girl's hand he led her to where his two horses stood.

'You ride on alone,' he said to his bride. 'I must invite guests to our wedding. Don't worry, I shall shortly overtake you by another track. But mind you follow my directions: as you travel along the eastern road you will come to a parting of the ways—to the east hangs a sable skin, to the west a bear skin. Take the turning by the sable and you will reach my home safely. Should you travel westwards you will come to the house of the daughter of the Devil Abaasy and meet a terrible fate!'

The fern girl adorned herself with fine jewels and dressed in velvet before setting off alone for her husband's home. As she rode along, happy in her thoughts of a contented life with her husband, she missed the parting of the ways and took the westward road marked by the bear skin. On and on she went until finally she

arrived at the house of the Devil's daughter.

'Old Baiberikeen's daughter is evidently on her way to the home of her husband, the son of Hara Haan,' muttered the Abaasy girl. 'And she has decided to pay me her respects on the way. Hey there, fern girl, come and rest in my house.'

The fern girl was too afraid to refuse and she followed the Abaasy girl into the house and sat down at the table, as she was bid. The Devil's daughter brought human flesh from the left and from the right of the room, and put it in a pot to boil. When the meal was ready, she set it before the fern girl who made as if she were eating, but thrust the boiled flesh quickly on to the floor.

'Ah, my dear,' said the Devil's daughter, 'I see old Baiberikeen has dressed you in fine clothes and beautiful jewellery. Take them off, my child, for me to try.'

The fern girl did as she was told.

When the Abaasy girl had put on the clothes and

jewels, she suddenly seized the maid by her hair, stripped the skin from off her head and face and put it over her own. Then she led her to the left and the fern girl felt she was walking on a dried skin; it gave way beneath her and she fell into a dark cellar.

Then, the Abaasy girl seated herself on the waiting horse and rode off to Hara Haan's house.

Meanwhile, in the bridegroom's camp, preparations were underway for the wedding ceremony. Meat was simmering in giant pots and all the eating vessels were being washed in the stream. Now and then, boys and girls would run out of Hara Haan's tent to watch out for the bride's coming.

'She's coming, she's coming!' they shouted at last, running into the tent.

Old Hara Haan then said wisely, 'Note well where the bride tethers her horse. If she is a good and able woman she will tie her horse to the last post; should she be bad and artful she will tie it to the first. Let us see.'

The bride arrived, dismounted and tethered her horse to the first post. Her husband came towards her and led her by the hand to his father's tent. And the wedding feast began.

At dusk the whole gathering lay down to sleep. The young man caressed his wife but her skin was hard and scaly.

'My dear, why is your skin so hard and scaly?' he asked.

'Oh, when I was small, old Baiberikeen made me wear a heavy necklace which rubbed against my skin and made it rough,' she replied.

Then the husband caressed his wife's head, and the head was hard and lumpy to his touch.

'My dear, why is your head so hard and lumpy?' he asked.

'Because my mother made me wear a heavy head-dress when I was young, and that creased and roughened my scalp,' she replied.

He touched his wife's hands and they were rough and crooked.

'My dear, why are your hands so rough and crooked?' he asked.

'Oh, my mother always put rings on my fingers and they wore down my hands,' she replied.

So the night went by and the days passed in the unfortunate household.

Whenever the new wife cooked a meal, the food turned sour; the taste was so unpleasant that the family could not eat it. The calves she tended grew hunched and died in their cribs. The little foals she fed grew crooked and died in their stables. When she went to milk the cows, their udders withered and became covered in sores and the milk turned sour. If she knitted anything, the garment came apart at the seams. All that she touched went awry.

With every day that passed, Hara Haan lost more animals. All that lived withered and he grew poorer and poorer.

In the meantime, not far from these misfortunes, lived old woman Baiberikeen, lonely as before. One night she had a dream: she dreamed that her dear daughter had lost her way, arrived at the house of the Devil's daughter and was even now lying in the cellar there. She tried to think of a meaning to her dream.

In the end she could not, so she set out for the house she had seen in her dream, and finally arrived there. But nobody was home. The fire on the hearth had gone out. The ash in the stove was cold. Yet from somewhere below she heard the faint sound of sobbing. To the left of the room old Baiberikeen suddenly noticed a hole and it was from there that the sounds of weeping came.

'Who is there?' she asked, peering down into the cellar.

'Mother, help me, pull me out,' came her daughter's voice. 'The Devil's daughter threw me down here; she took my clothes, my hair and the skin of my face, put them all on herself and rode off on my horse. Help me out, Mother.'

The old woman fetched a rope, let it down and pulled up her daughter from the cellar. Together they returned home and it was not long before the girl had quite recovered and was even more lovely than before.

Now it came to the ears of Hara Haan, told to him by his dappled mare, that old Baiberikeen had another daughter. So the father told his son this news and put to him the following question, 'My son, do you know the origin of your woman?'

And the son replied, 'There is in the upper world, beyond the third sky, a younger brother of the White

Creator Lord who collects all the migrating birds. It was his daughters, the seven maidens that turned into seven cranes, who came down to a round meadow and danced upon the earth. And with them came their nurse, the Lady Jayehait who chose the best of the seven cranes and said, "You are to remain in this unclean middle world; you are destined for the son of Hara Haan, you will become a human, bear children and tend cattle." With that the nurse cut off her wings.

'Of course, the maiden wept and pleaded. But it was no use. "Turn into a fern and grow," said the nurse. "The old woman, mistress of five cows, will find the fern and, once you have turned into a human child and grown up, she will wed you to the son of Hara Haan."

'So I took what was destined to be mine. And now I must live with her despite her evil ways.'

But his father urged him to pay another visit to Old Baiberikeen to see her new daughter.

So the young man said to his wife, 'Let us go and pay your mother a visit.'

'Why should we travel so far? And at harvest time,' she objected. 'I certainly will not go.'

Several times he tried to persuade her and at last she gave in reluctantly. Having prepared some gifts, the son-in-law and his wife set out to visit the old woman. They arrived to find the mother and her new daughter at home.

As soon as he set eyes on Baiberikeen's new daughter, the young man was astonished to find that her face and beauty were exactly those of the maid he had sought to marry. Looking from her to his wife, he now saw how ugly his wife had become.

They had their supper and were about to lie down to sleep when Baiberikeen's new daughter said she would like to tell a story.

'Keep your stories to yourself,' said the Abaasy girl. 'I'm tired.' And she pretended to fall asleep.

'Well then, sleep,' her husband said, 'and we'll listen to the story. Please proceed with your tale.'

'Not many days past,' the fern girl began, 'a handsome young man took a bride. Seating her upon a horse, he sent her on alone, himself riding by another route to invite friends to the wedding. But the girl, instead of travelling straight to her new home, missed her turning

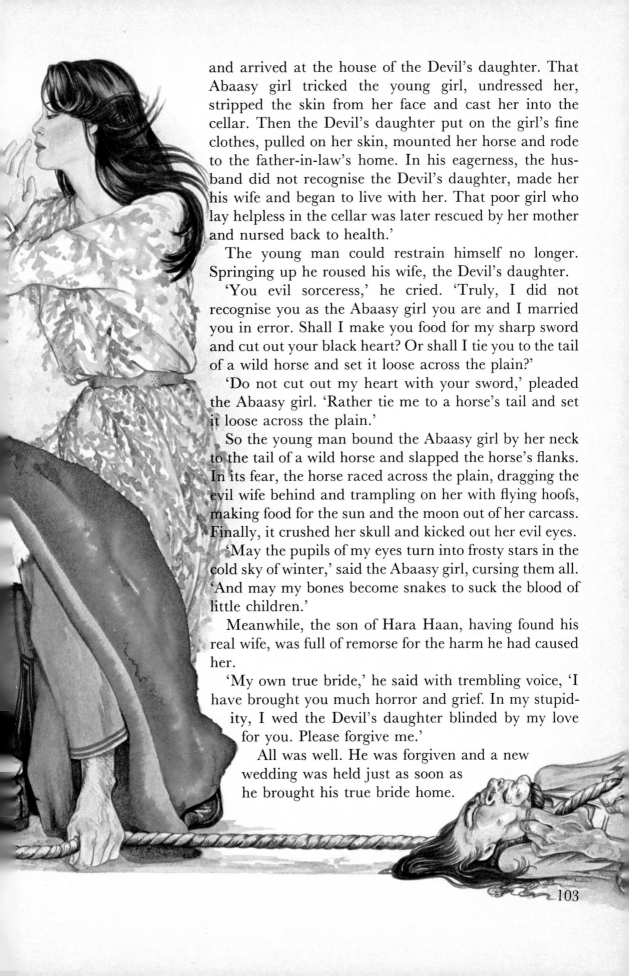

and arrived at the house of the Devil's daughter. That
Abaasy girl tricked the young girl, undressed her,
stripped the skin from her face and cast her into the
cellar. Then the Devil's daughter put on the girl's fine
clothes, pulled on her skin, mounted her horse and rode
to the father-in-law's home. In his eagerness, the husband did not recognise the Devil's daughter, made her
his wife and began to live with her. That poor girl who
lay helpless in the cellar was later rescued by her mother
and nursed back to health.'

The young man could restrain himself no longer.
Springing up he roused his wife, the Devil's daughter.

'You evil sorceress,' he cried. 'Truly, I did not
recognise you as the Abaasy girl you are and I married
you in error. Shall I make you food for my sharp sword
and cut out your black heart? Or shall I tie you to the tail
of a wild horse and set it loose across the plain?'

'Do not cut out my heart with your sword,' pleaded
the Abaasy girl. 'Rather tie me to a horse's tail and set
it loose across the plain.'

So the young man bound the Abaasy girl by her neck
to the tail of a wild horse and slapped the horse's flanks.
In its fear, the horse raced across the plain, dragging the
evil wife behind and trampling on her with flying hoofs,
making food for the sun and the moon out of her carcass.
Finally, it crushed her skull and kicked out her evil eyes.

'May the pupils of my eyes turn into frosty stars in the
cold sky of winter,' said the Abaasy girl, cursing them all.
'And may my bones become snakes to suck the blood of
little children.'

Meanwhile, the son of Hara Haan, having found his
real wife, was full of remorse for the harm he had caused
her.

'My own true bride,' he said with trembling voice, 'I
have brought you much horror and grief. In my stupid-
ity, I wed the Devil's daughter blinded by my love
for you. Please forgive me.'

All was well. He was forgiven and a new
wedding was held just as soon as
he brought his true bride home.

Heesi's Millstone

At the edge of the Karelian forest where the firs and larches sweep down to the White Sea, there stands a village of neat wooden cottages. From inside a cottage one Christmastide came the sound of children crying. It was the home of a poor fisherman who had no food to feed his seven children. In despair, his wife sent him to beg for food at the house of a rich cousin, at the other end of the village.

When he came to the house and the cousin came to the door, the poor man said, 'Give me a little meat for Christmas, cousin. My children are starving.'

The rich man roughly thrust a cow's hoof into the poor fisherman's hands and he, poor soul, fell to his knees in grateful thanks. Yet that only angered the host, who was pained enough at having to part even with the hoof.

'Get you gone, scrounger!' he shouted. 'And don't come back. To the Devil with you!'

Away shuffled the poor fisherman with his cow's hoof and a frown upon his brow.

'So be it, if my cousin says so,' he mumbled to himself. 'I'll have to go to the Devil then. But where am I to find him?'

He wandered into the forest and followed a beaten track until he caught the sound of woodmen at their work.

'Hey, woodmen,' he called, 'do you know the way to the Devil?'

'Sure we do,' they answered. 'Though if you take our advice you'll keep well clear of him. The Devil is Heesi, an ogre, twenty-two feet tall and master of this forest. What do you want with him?'

'It's like this,' explained the poor man. 'My cousin, God bless him, has sent me to the Devil with a cow's hoof. So I have to find him.'

'If go you must,' they said, 'then follow the trail of our felled trees, for we are the Devil's woodcutters; you'll come to his house soon enough. But listen well: take with you a stout birch log, for as you enter his house he will go to shake your hand. Give him the birchwood log instead or he'll turn your hand to mincemeat. One thing more— should he offer you a reward, ask for nothing save his magic millstone. He keeps it hanging behind him on the wall. Do that and you'll never want for food again.'

Thanking the woodmen for their advice, the poor man

went on his way through the forest until he came to Heesi's house. With a polite knock he opened the stout pine door, walked boldly in and stood before a tall stone stove. He was much afraid of the sight that met him. There on the stove sat the old ogre, his white hair and beard flowing to the floor, a single yellow tooth hanging over his bottom lip, his brown gnarled hands broader even than the oldest tree.

The poor fisherman stared about him nervously as Heesi stretched out his enormous hand and boomed, 'Welcome Guest!'

Thereupon the fisherman thrust his stout birch log into Heesi's outstretched hand—and straightaway sawdust ran through the ogre's giant fingers.

The poor man stared. 'I've brought you a gift,' he stuttered. 'A cow's hoof.'

Old Heesi smiled. Taking the hoof he crunched it contentedly with his gums and swallowed it down, not leaving a scrap of bone or gristle.

'Many promise me food,' he wheezed, 'but none dare come near my forest home. Sometimes they send their hounds with meaty bones for me, but the greedy animals eat them on the way. Now, what will you take as your reward—gold or silver?'

'I've no use for gold or silver,' said the poor man. 'But if you wish to reward me, give me that millstone hanging at your back.'

Old Heesi's smile soon disappeared. He had no wish to part with his magic millstone; so he offered a pot of gold, a tub of silver, a chest of salt. All to no avail. The poor man was as stubborn as he was simple, and refused them all.

'Ah well,' Heesi sighed at last, 'I suppose I must grant you what you ask: take the millstone, but mind one thing, this is no ordinary millstone. Just say, "Grind my millstone, grind away!" and it will bring you what you wish. And when you've had enough, just tell it, "Enough and have done, my millstone!" and it will stop. Now be off with you before I change my mind.'

The poor fisherman took the magic millstone and set off for home with it slung across his shoulders. As he reached the cottage door, he saw his angry wife waiting for him, hands on hips, the children bawling loudly.

'Where have you been, you good-for-nothing hus-

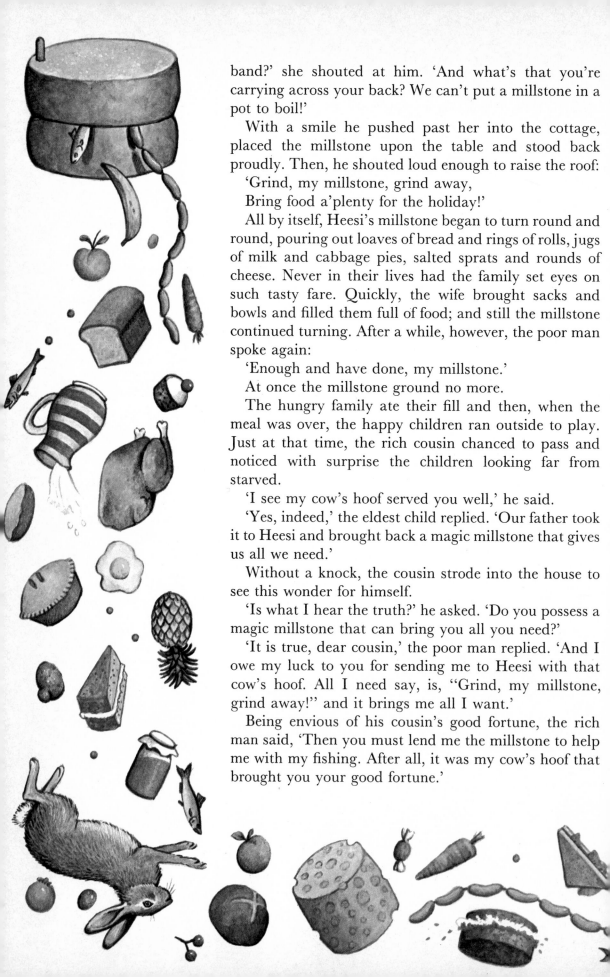

band?' she shouted at him. 'And what's that you're carrying across your back? We can't put a millstone in a pot to boil!'

With a smile he pushed past her into the cottage, placed the millstone upon the table and stood back proudly. Then, he shouted loud enough to raise the roof:

'Grind, my millstone, grind away,
Bring food a'plenty for the holiday!'

All by itself, Heesi's millstone began to turn round and round, pouring out loaves of bread and rings of rolls, jugs of milk and cabbage pies, salted sprats and rounds of cheese. Never in their lives had the family set eyes on such tasty fare. Quickly, the wife brought sacks and bowls and filled them full of food; and still the millstone continued turning. After a while, however, the poor man spoke again:

'Enough and have done, my millstone.'

At once the millstone ground no more.

The hungry family ate their fill and then, when the meal was over, the happy children ran outside to play. Just at that time, the rich cousin chanced to pass and noticed with surprise the children looking far from starved.

'I see my cow's hoof served you well,' he said.

'Yes, indeed,' the eldest child replied. 'Our father took it to Heesi and brought back a magic millstone that gives us all we need.'

Without a knock, the cousin strode into the house to see this wonder for himself.

'Is what I hear the truth?' he asked. 'Do you possess a magic millstone that can bring you all you need?'

'It is true, dear cousin,' the poor man replied. 'And I owe my luck to you for sending me to Heesi with that cow's hoof. All I need say, is, "Grind, my millstone, grind away!" and it brings me all I want.'

Being envious of his cousin's good fortune, the rich man said, 'Then you must lend me the millstone to help me with my fishing. After all, it was my cow's hoof that brought you your good fortune.'

Readily the simple-hearted man agreed. However, such was the greedy cousin's haste that he clean forgot to ask the words that stopped the millstone grinding.

He hurried down to the sea with his load, set it in the bows of his boat and headed out to sea. When he was already far from shore, he cast his nets into the water and soon pulled in a heavy catch. Not satisfied with this, the greedy man resolved to salt the fish without delay. Standing up in his boat, he yelled above the wind:

'Grind, my millstone, grind away,
Pour out salt the livelong day!'

The millstone at once began to spin and turn, grinding out the purest, whitest salt. There was soon enough to salt the whole boatload of teeming fish. The rich cousin looked on in glee, rubbing his hands and smacking his lips. But the salt continued to pour out: more and more and more in a never-ending stream. Soon his greedy smile turned into an anxious frown. It was now high time to halt the millstone, but what were the words to use?

'Stop, my millstone, stop, stop, stop!'
'Grind no more and go to sleep!'
'Enough, enough, enough, I say!'

It was no use.

So heavy was the boat by now that it was steadily sinking deeper into the water. Soon the sea was coming over the sides of the boat and it was near to capsizing altogether. With a desperate effort, the old miser tried to pick up the millstone and cast it overboard. Yet it seemed stuck fast to the deck, and would not move.

'Help me! Help me, someone!' he bawled in panic. But there was no one near to hear his cries. As the sea closed over his final shouts, the rich man, with his boat and fish, sank down to the bottom of the ocean.

What of Heesi's millstone? The fisherfolk who dwell upon these shores will tell you that even on the sea bed it continued turning, turning, turning. And it remains there still, grinding out an endless stream of salt.

That is why, if you have not already guessed, the sea is always salt.

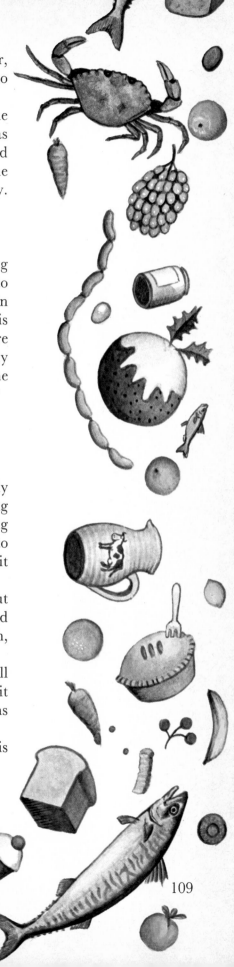

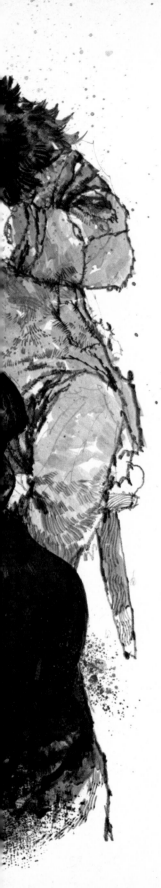

The Devil's Gauntlet

'Now I'm going to spin you the finest of yarns, one of mystery and fear. And if there's any among you who have a mind to run the Devil's Gauntlet or meet a werewolf, you had better listen carefully. Before I start my story I shall make the sign of the cross to keep the Devil and his demons at bay. I had enough of those evil villains in my younger days. . . .'

Not a man stirred. They all huddled closer round the wood-stove where the cook was getting ready to tell a tale fit for the occasion. It was New Year's Eve in the year 1858, in the depths of the virgin forests at the head of the Gatineau River in Canada. The winter had been hard and the snows already reached up to the cabin roofs in the Ross lumber camp.

The camp boss had ordered the customary small barrel of rum to be shared among the lumberjacks, and the cook had already prepared the pancakes and jack-rabbit stew for New Year's Day. Bubbling in a big pot was the molasses for the toffee-pulling party which was to bring the evening to a close.

Every man present had filled his pipe with good Canadian tobacco, and a thick cloud of smoke darkened the inside of the log cabin. The crackling fire of resinous pine cast a flickering red glow upon the rugged faces of those hardy workers.

Joe the cook was a small, humpbacked man who had been working the camps for a good forty years. He'd seen a thing or two in his colourful life, and it only needed a tot of rum to loosen his tongue and get him to recount his adventures. So now he cleared his throat, spat into the stove and began the story in his rough, nasal tones.

'Did you ever hear the name of Baptiste Durant? Now there was a man as tough as an old buck moose—a big, black-bearded fellow with a voice as strong as his own two arms. When Baptiste came into a lumber camp it would be one big fist-in-the-face fight after another. Good thing he spent most of his time in the wilds with his trap lines and sled dogs. Perhaps that's how he came to run the Devil's Gauntlet and meet a werewolf at the same time.

'Every winter Baptiste Durant went up north where the fur grew thickest and the snow lay deepest. He would take his team of five dogs up to the top of the world, where the northern lights dangle on coloured strings like dancing puppets.

'One time, old Baptiste made camp for the night as usual. He carefully counted out the otter and fox hides on the sled before turning the dogs loose and cutting down some fir branches for their beds. After throwing them some half-frozen fish, he set to making up his own bed. He was dog-tired, old Baptiste, and would soon be sleeping like a log.

'But scarcely had the trapper closed his eyes when he heard a hoarse sing-song chanting coming from somewhere above his head:

> "Ma ne mi ne ma ne mo,
> On we go, boys, on we go.
> Ma ne mi ne ma ne mo,
> Ma ne mi ne ma ne mo."

'He opened his eyes and saw in the sky a long birch-bark canoe with eight men in it paddling along as they sang their song.

'"The Devil's Gauntlet!" thought Baptiste at once. He had once heard a crazy story about this canoe of the north: it was said to carry the souls of dead trappers returning for a last look at their homes and loved ones. They were carried along by the Devil himself—or so folk said. Mind, if a Frenchman fresh from France saw the canoe, he would cry, "La chasse galerie! Look at the huntsmen riding through the sky on their horses." That's because Frenchmen fresh from France can't tell a canoe from a horse and are unhandy with the ways of the Canadian forest!

'By this time Baptiste's dogs were awake and began their wolf-like howling at the apparition in the sky, "Hurroolll . . . Hurroolll. . . ."

'What with the hounds howling and the dead men chanting it was enough to knock the lid off the trapper's head—worse than ten tots of good Jamaican rum. Baptiste had heard, too, that the Devil was ever on the look out for more paddlers for his canoe. And he who chanced to run the Devil's Gauntlet was doomed unless he could travel faster than the dead souls could paddle.

'The trapper decided to break camp and hit the trail as fast as he possibly could. The sky was almost as light as day with the northern lights glimmering in their blue and red and yellow stripes as backdrop to the scene. He called his dogs to harness, and in an instant four had shaken off the snow and come to heel; only the old lead dog Loup did not come to his call. Baptiste cursed his luck and began searching in the snow for the lazy hound.

'There were grey mounds sticking up through the white snow, and Baptiste went from one to another, kicking them hard to see if the mound was his dog Loup. Finally he found him—one furry white mound leapt up snarling at the boot that had disturbed its slumbers. Baptiste brought his whip down hard on the dog's savage head.

'"You bad-tempered cur!" he shouted. "Get yourself to the sled before I kick the stuffing out of you!"

'Yet the beast only snarled more fiercely than ever and, in its ugly dream-shattered mood, leapt at the trapper's throat.

'"What's gotten into you Loup?" roared Baptiste.

'Throwing down his whip, he grabbed hold of the animal's long grey muzzle. With his right hand he seized its top jaw, with his left he caught its bottom jaw. Then he ground the fangs together and held them shut while the enraged beast kicked and squirmed.

'"I'll teach you to try to bite old Baptiste," said the trapper. "You'll do as I command."

'He let go of the animal's muzzle and quickly snatched up his whip. As he brought the whip down hard on the animal's back, it let out a long, pained growl and turned to run off. Before it could get far, Baptiste caught it by the tail and pulled it back through the snow. Then he picked it up and with his brawny arms began to swing it

round and round. The beast yelped and howled and soon was completely dizzy. Only then did the master take it by the nape of its rough fur neck and drag it to the sled.

The other dogs were agitated by the arrival of their leader. They all howled and sprang on one another until they were all as tangled and quarrelsome as ten wolves with one jack rabbit. Cursing loudly, Baptiste brought the handle of his whip down hard on each one in turn and soon had them straightened out and straining in their harness. That done, he walked to the back of the sled and took a firm grip on its handles. With a darting

glance up at the Devil's Canoe, he roared at the top of his voice, "Allez-allez. Mush, Mush! You black-hearted beasts. Allez, Loup, you wretched layabout. Get cracking before the Devil has us for his boat."

'The savage leader took off as if he knew the Devil was on his tail. So did the other dogs behind him. Pou-i-i-iche! The sled rushed along like the roaring wind, and Baptiste could hardly touch the ground with his flying feet.

'"Whoa!" he cried. "Not so fast. You'll overturn the sled. What's got into you all of a sudden?"

'Glancing over his shoulder to see whether anything had shaken loose from the sled, he noticed a dark grey shadow following them across the white snow. Was it the Devil in the shape of a wolf? No wonder the dogs were in such a haste.

'"A werewolf!" cried the trapper. "Mush! Mush!"

'He cracked his whip over the five dogs, urging them

115

on even faster. The sled hurtled over the snow, bumping over hummocks and rocking first on one runner, then on the other. At any moment it seemed the sled would crash, sending the trapper flying into the snow. Up above them the dead men paddled faster and faster. Everyone seemed to be in frenzied flight from the werewolf chasing the sled.

'"On, Loup, on," shouted Baptiste, cracking his whip hard on the leader's back.

'That lead dog needed no urging. It raced over the snow like a silver streak, pulling the sled and the other four dogs in its wake. All the same, the werewolf was gaining on them.

'As the beast came nearer and nearer, the trapper realised they could not escape. The heavy sled with its fox and otter pelts was no match for the fleet-footed beast behind them.

'With a despairing shout, Baptiste called the sled dogs to a halt and hauled hard on the sled ropes. As the sled faltered in the snow, he snatched up his gun and pointed it at the werewolf which was almost on him.

'"Bang!" went the gun, but the movements of the Devil's Canoe above him spoiled the trapper's aim and blurred his sight. He missed the beast once, and he missed again. Before he could fire once more, that werewolf was at his throat.

'Baptiste was thrown to the ground, and had all the breath and strength knocked out of him. He knew it must be the end and he would soon be taking his place in the Devil's Canoe.

'The furry beast buried its claws in his chest and he could feel its hot breath on his neck, see its yellow fangs. He closed his eyes.

'But then—name of the Devil!—the beast began to lick his black-bearded face, as if kissing him in relief and delight.

'Opening his eyes, the trapper suddenly shouted with joy, "Loup! It's Loup. You old son-of-a-gun!"

'And he embraced his old lead dog as one snatched from the jaws of death. But then, in the midst of these celebrations, he suddenly sat up and stared at his five sled dogs. Yes, all five were present and the leader was sitting there patiently, waiting for the next command.

'"If you're not a werewolf—you're old Loup, then who

on earth is that in your place?"

'All of a sudden it came to him. "Loup garou—a wild wolf!" he shouted. "My God, I've hitched a wild wolf to my sled. . . .""

'Springing up, he grabbed his gun again and pointed it at the head of the big grey wolf. He looked down the long barrel of his gun into those grey-flecked, yellow eyes. "Why didn't I notice those yellow eyes before?" he thought. Then he looked at the wolf's friendly grin spreading upwards from his long grey snout and he hesitated.

'Baptiste Durant dropped his gun to his side. He unhitched the wolf and put Loup back in his place. With a friendly ruffling of the wolf's grey neck fur, Baptiste pushed the wolf away towards the forest.

'"Be gone," he said with a chuckle, "and take your grey hide with you before I add it to the fox and otter hides in the sled."

'Just at that moment, he heard once more the incessant chanting of the dead men:

> "Ma ne mi ne ma ne mo,
> On we go, boys, on we go.
> Ma ne mi ne ma ne mo,
> Ma ne mi ne ma ne mo."

'Baptiste again drove off like the wind, followed closely by the Devil's Canoe with the dead men paddling hard to keep up with him. The chase continued all through the night and it was only as the northern lights began to dim that the Devil's Canoe sped off faster and faster until it vanished over the top of the world.

'"Galloping caribou!" cried Baptiste with relief, bringing his sled to a halt. "I can't believe what has happened this night. I've run the Devil's Gauntlet and lived to tell the tale. I've hitched a wild wolf to my sled and still have my hide intact. All that in one night."

'He was a lucky man. Very few trappers have run the Devil's Gauntlet with the help of a wild wolf and lived to tell the tale!'

Joe the cook plunged the wooden spoon into the boiling pot of golden molasses and, after a long silence, announced that since the toffee was ready for pulling they should go right ahead and pull it.

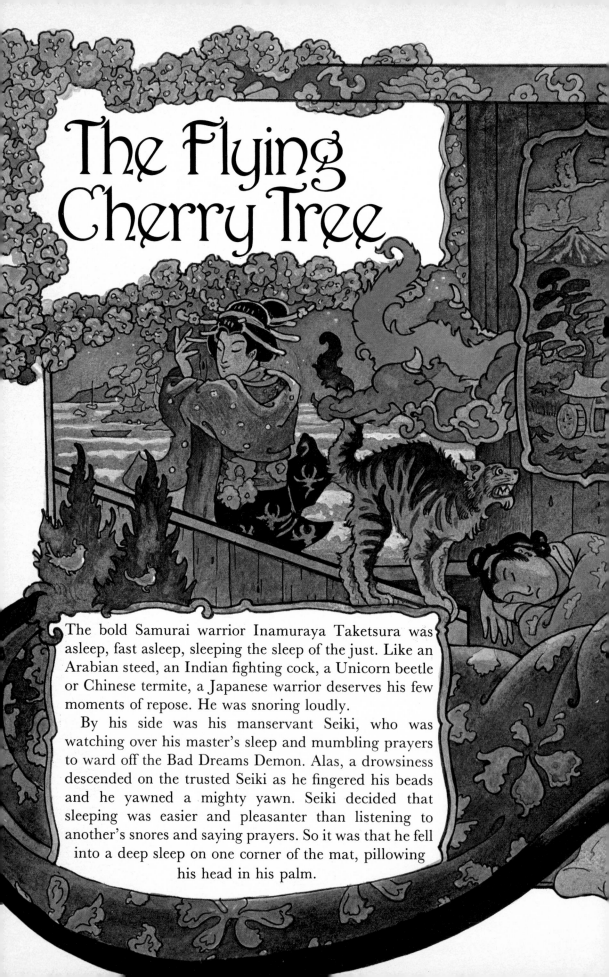

The Flying Cherry Tree

The bold Samurai warrior Inamuraya Taketsura was asleep, fast asleep, sleeping the sleep of the just. Like an Arabian steed, an Indian fighting cock, a Unicorn beetle or Chinese termite, a Japanese warrior deserves his few moments of repose. He was snoring loudly.

By his side was his manservant Seiki, who was watching over his master's sleep and mumbling prayers to ward off the Bad Dreams Demon. Alas, a drowsiness descended on the trusted Seiki as he fingered his beads and he yawned a mighty yawn. Seiki decided that sleeping was easier and pleasanter than listening to another's snores and saying prayers. So it was that he fell into a deep sleep on one corner of the mat, pillowing his head in his palm.

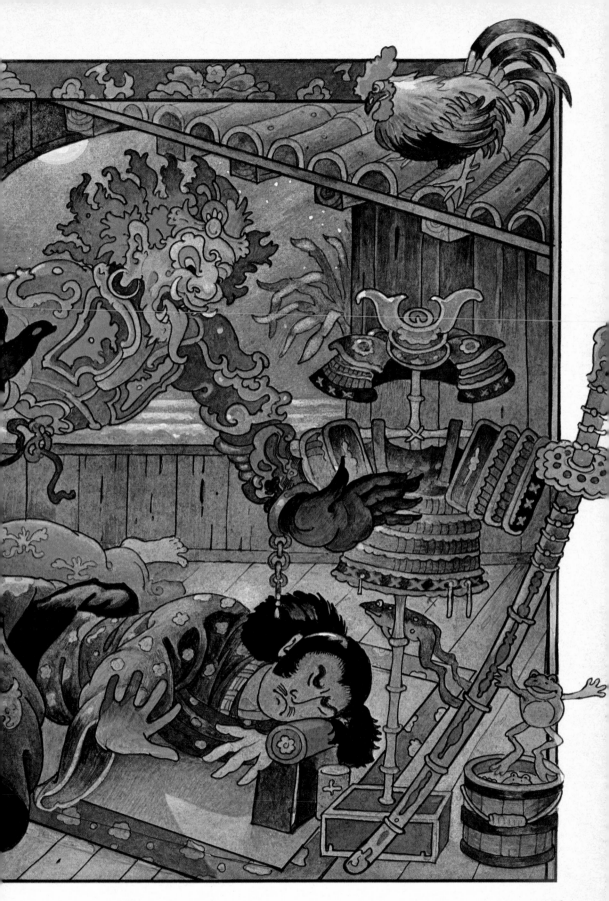

Now there came the fatal moment. From behind a painting on the wall, on which were drawn Fujiyama Mountain and, close by, a water mill and, not far off, a flock of cranes flying south, peeped the Bad Dreams Demon. He spied the master and servant doing their best to imitate the water mill grinding and the cranes hooting as they flew by Fujiyama.

Grinning broadly, that demon descended on the two sleepers. First he hid Seiki's beads, then he paced round the room peering here and there; when he stared into the water pail, toads and tadpoles at once appeared in the water!

Then the Bad Dreams Demon shook the bushy tip of his tail under Inamuraya's nose and said with an evil chuckle, 'This bold Samurai must have swallowed a good dozen drums to create such a clamour in his belly. Could it be that his left nostril conceals the typhoon that recently transported Koshiki Shima Island ninety-nine shi into the air? Sleep on, sleep on, son of earthquake and cyclone. I shall sprinkle some dust from my tail into your nose and give you such a horrible dream that I wouldn't even wish it on a yard-dog barking at the moon!'

Having made good his intention he flew off in a hurry. But as he rushed away, his tail tipped the picture of Fujiyama Mountain upside down so that the poor bewildered cranes knew not where to fly.

Before Seiki fell asleep and the Bad Dreams Demon arrived, the warrior Inamuraya had been having a lovely dream. He had been dreaming that he had crossed the Yellow Sea, conquered the entire celestial empire, built an enormous ship, put on board it the great city of Beiping with its emperor's palace and all its houses big and small, and was now sailing back to the Land of the Rising Sun.

This wonderful dream voyage was almost at an end when Inamuraya decided once again to count his Chinese prisoners. All the Chinese sat in the ship's hold tied to one another by their pigtails, much resembling bunches of bananas. Their feet were locked in wooden stocks on which they were drumming with their toes and, Inamuraya thought, a very pleasant music resulted.

Inamuraya had scarcely managed to count to three million, seven hundred thousand, one hundred and eleven, when all of a sudden he lost count.

Something was tickling his nose and making him want to sneeze. Of course, he knew full well he must not sneeze in the prison hold, for if he did the entire ship would be blown apart and it would sink to the bottom of the sea. Thus, falling over the Chinese in his hurry, Inamuraya rushed up to the deck.

It was precisely at that moment that his bad dream started.

The Chinese suddenly leapt up, rubbed their heads together so that their pigtails came undone, flung off the wooden stocks and dashed after Inamuraya. They seized his legs just as he was climbing on to the deck, pulled him back into the hold, took down his trousers, made a cat-o'-nine-tails out of their pigtails and ... Well, poor Inamuraya never did tell of the terrible shame that those wretched Chinamen brought upon him.

At last the bold Samurai could bear it no longer. He let out a loud cry and sneezed such a mighty sneeze that the whole ship burst asunder. A water spout rose up, shooting Inamuraya so far and so high that he landed right in his own room. Squatting on his haunches, he sneezed again and again. Opposite him, also on his haunches, was Seiki who, in turn, also sneezed and almost hit the ceiling. A few grains of dust from the Bad Dreams Demon's tail had naturally come his way too.

Both men leapt on one another like fighting cocks until with a final 'aitchoo' their heads banged together with a mighty thud.

'A curse on all Chinese!' yelled Inamuraya as he scrambled to his feet. 'What a nightmare!'

Reaching for the water pail to pour himself a drink, he saw the toads hopping and the tadpoles swimming in the water. In a fury, he seized his sword and brought it down hard on the pail, smashing it to pieces and scattering the water everywhere. At once the toads hopped out of the door and the tadpoles turned to drops of water as if they had never been.

With that the spell was broken. But Inamuraya Taketsura was angry twice over: for the loss of a good dream as much as for the bad dream. Though he frowned hard he could not recall the valiant battles, or his conquest of the celestial empire, or the great city of Beiping which he had carried off on his ship. It had all flown from his head like a pink dragonfly out of the

121

window. He was very angry.

'I'll swallow my sword if I don't cut off someone's head,' he vowed. 'In fact, I will cut off the head of the first person to enter this room.'

Now you should know, good readers, that the vow of a Samurai was something sacred; and it *had* to be kept.

At the sound of her father's voice, the lovely O Tai entered the room.

The young maiden was of an age when girls are likened to flowers: some to lotus blossom, some to carnations, some to snowdrops, some to mignonettes, some to briar roses and some to chrysanthemums. O Tai was likened to cherry blossom.

As she entered, she asked her father, 'Has someone disturbed your dreams, honourable Father? You curse loud enough to wake the dead.'

'O luckless one!' shouted Inamuraya. 'Your curiosity will cost you dear.'

Uncomprehending, the lovely O Tai stared at her father as he spat on his sword and wiped it with his palm.

'I must cut off your head,' Inamuraya said. 'That was the vow I made.'

'Surely you would not remove my pretty head,' said O Tai. 'If you did, I should not be able to hear the birds singing in the garden; I should not see the gold-tipped butterflies which settle on my kimono; I should not be able to kiss your prickly burdock cheeks as an honourable daughter should.'

'But I have given my word, O Tai,' her father solemnly said. 'It must be done.'

O Tai appealed once more, saying, 'Then no more would I see my dear cherry tree that grows beside our house. I love it as my own good mother. At dusk I bring water to it from the canal. I tie its boughs with silk threads so that they can bear the weight of the fruit. In winter I surround its roots with straw mats so that they do not freeze. See how beautiful it is now, covered in pink blossom.'

And turning to the cherry tree beside the door, O Tai called, 'Dear cherry tree, please protect me.'

As Inamuraya lifted the sword above his daughter's head, the cherry tree suddenly spread its branches through the door, snatched up the lovely maiden, tore up its roots from the soil and, showering Inamuraya's head

with earth, flew up and away across the rooftops.

'Stop, stop,' shouted Inamuraya. 'I must keep my word.'

With that he jumped up and struck at the cherry tree as it passed overhead. He only succeeded in cutting off a blossom-covered bough and that fell upon his head, showering him with petals that clogged his mouth, ears and nostrils. He was so enraged that his mind was closed to the lines of the immortal bard:

"The breath of a cherry tree
    In blossom is like a gentle smile
    That sometimes blossoms
    Upon a loved one's lips."

Meanwhile the flying cherry tree winged its way northwards towards Nagasaki, then turned east and soon came down on the deserted island of Tsushima. Here O Tai lived for three whole years. The provident cherry tree really did become like a mother to her and fulfilled all her needs. The three years passed in carefree happiness and O Tai would have lived many more years contentedly on the desert island had not two fishermen sailed by in a red boat one evening. They were taking plaice and squid to market in Nagasaki and debating all the latest news.

'This year is full of news,' one was saying. 'The emperor died of cholera. An earthquake destroyed the town of Yedo. Three Samurais in Hakodate had an argument over who could eat a live shark, but the shark swallowed all three. In Kyushu, some monks stole a silver statue of Buddha from a temple so as to sell it to monks in Kiobashi who melted it down to make saki goblets; now both sets of monks have silver on their hands which they cannot wash off.'

The other fisherman took up the news, saying, 'No rice was grown on Hondo this year, so the poor are baking loaves from clay. At Moji a peasant dared to eat the dung that a Daimio's horse had left on the road—and he was buried alive in punishment. Do you know that the head priest at the Saihodja temple in Nagasaki claims that the soul of one of his ancestors resides in a plaice? He might take all our fish from us without paying.'

The first man spoke up again: 'I've heard tell that the

bold Samurai Inamuraya Taketsura is very ill; he who had a dream more horrid than can be recalled in the Land of the Rising Sun. In three days he will be dead unless he can appease the Sickness Demon. To do that, a near relative must cut off one of their hands and give it to him—such was the verdict of the eminent physician who is attending him. All the same, none of his relatives seem in a hurry to lose a hand.'

The fisherman sailed on, out of earshot of O Tai.

The young maiden was in great distress as she pressed her lovely face against the cherry tree.

'Gentle Mother, what am I to do?' she cried. 'Who will bear my hand to my poor father? Oh dear, why did I not stop the fishermen in their red boat and sail with them back to my father?'

The cherry tree's branches drooped in sadness.

'Have you not been happy with me these past three years, O Tai?' it asked.

'Oh yes, Mother,' cried O Tai. 'I was happy just as long as there was no demand for plaice and squid in Nagasaki; not a single fishing boat sailed by our island in all that time, so I knew nothing of my dear father's sickness. Dear Mother, let us return home quickly.'

O Tai threw her arms round the cherry tree, and kissed the silvery bark on which time's painless chisel had etched her gentle lines. If you looked closely at the bark you could read in these lines the poetry of those whom fate had sat in the tree's consoling shade. Just above O Tai's head were lines inscribed many years before; she had often wondered at their meaning:

> "In meadows and groves
> I catch the spring breeze.
> Love, tarry awhile,
> Fly not so fast
> In the fleeting spring breeze."

'How strange are mortals,' sighed the cherry tree. 'They are good and evil, foolish and wise, irate and mild, lazy and busy, yet very rarely happy. Not from anything do they run so fast as from happiness.'

Nevertheless, speaking softly to the young maiden, the tree said, 'Very well, O Tai, let it be as you wish.'

Thereupon O Tai found herself sitting in the

topmost branches of the tree and flying with the ease of a lark towards the east.

At this very time the bold Samurai Inamuraya Taketsura was lying on his death bed, groaning softly and demanding his sharp sword to fight off the Sickness Demon. Around him sat the mourners and his embarrassed relatives.

'The sword is under your left side,' said the physician, busy preparing one hundred and thirteen different medicines in one hundred and thirteen different bottles.

'My sword is heavier than a mountain,' murmured Inamuraya. 'I cannot lift it.'

At that, all the mourners left the room, making way for Death who was impatiently knocking on the ceiling. Then, from under the rush mat, on which the physician had been sitting, crawled the Sickness Demon. He leaned over the Samurai and waved a fiery fan before his face. The sick man heard his voice crackling like withered leaves swept up by the autumn wind.

'Your end is nigh, Samurai Inamuraya Taketsura. You have but sixteen more breaths before I close your throat forever,' said the Demon.

Just at that moment a gust of wind rattled the rooftiles and the servant Seiki could be heard shouting, 'Our cherry tree that flew away has now returned.'

The Sickness Demon rushed about willy-nilly, not knowing where to hide.

Inamuraya sat up in bed and sniffed the air. 'What a fragrant scent of cherry blossom,' he said. 'I can breathe more easily now. Does that mean I am already dead?'

'Master,' cried Seiki, 'the cherry tree has brought you back your health.' And Seiki bustled into the room with a pannet of cherry blossom on top of which lay the graceful white hand of O Tai.

Inamuraya jumped out of bed and ran to meet O Tai. 'At last you've returned!' he shouted joyfully. Then, with a swish of his sharp sword, he cut off her head; it lay at his feet like a still-ripening forest berry.

'So, my vow is kept,' he cried. 'Now, cut down that rebellious cherry tree and burn it at once.'

While the flying cherry tree was being cut down and burnt, the bold Samurai warrior Inamuraya Taketsura issued one more order: to send to Kyoto for the best scribe to write down this story.

The Demon of Stone Mountain

In the highlands of Tonkin in Vietnam there lived two brothers whose mother and father died in quick succession. A funeral was held, and while the younger brother was away burying his parents, the elder stayed at home to settle the inheritance. And he, being very greedy, concealed all there was of value.

When the younger brother returned, he looked about him in surprise.

'Tell me, honoured brother,' he asked, 'where is our parents' fortune? I see nothing of it here.'

'It is as your eyes behold,' replied the other. 'Our much-lamented parents left nothing save this empty house. Since I've a wife and you have none, the house shall remain with me.'

Thus it was. The elder brother took for himself the house, the entire family fortune, the rice fields and the oxen. To the young lad was left nothing but a small

maize strip in the foothills of Stone Mountain. And, besides, an old dog and cat.

The lad said not a word. Bowing low before his brother, he set off with his two animals to work the strip of maize. But how was he to till the land? He had no ox, no horse, no goat, no ass. His mangy dog and cat looked on in silent curiosity. He scratched his head, then with a shrug of his shoulders he hitched the two miserable animals to his plough and urged them forward. The dog howled, the cat wailed, and the plough wobbled on across the strip of maize. What a funny sight it was!

Looking down on this odd scene all the while was the Demon of Stone Mountain himself. He gazed down upon the fields and was unable to contain himself any longer: he shook his fat sides, wrinkled up his nose and opened wide his great stone mouth. How he chuckled at the strange spectacle.

Alarmed by the strange rumbling coming from the mountain, the lad looked up and caught his breath. For in the depths of that cavernous mouth he saw a store of glittering gold and silver. At once he left his plough and began to clamber up the mountainside, over the rocky chins and lips, until he reached the inside of the mouth. There he filled his sack with gold and silver, as much as he could carry. He escaped just in time as the stone mouth banged tightly shut.

Unable to believe his good fortune, the lad returned to the village with his precious load, and summoned craftsmen to build him a modest dwelling at the foot of Stone Mountain. Purchasing besides two prime oxen and a paddy field to grow some rice, he settled down with his dog and cat to live a life of modest contentment.

But no sooner did the elder brother learn of this good fortune than his heart filled with greed and envy. Calling one day upon his younger brother, he enquired how it was he had come to prosper so. The dutiful brother told his story, holding nothing back.

Thereupon, the greedy one set out for Stone Mountain with his wife, and the faithful dog and cat. He also took along two oxen carts on which to load the gold and silver.

When he arrived at the strip of maize in the foothills of the mountain, the older brother hitched the dog and cat to the plough, as his younger brother had described. Then he whipped them forward across the stony strip. The dog howled, the cat wailed and the Demon of Stone Mountain laughed so heartily that his fat sides shook like jelly, his big nose wrinkled and his great stone mouth gaped open wide. The treasure glinted brightly in the

depths of his cavernous mouth.

Casting the plough aside, the man and his wife rushed forward, clambered up the mountainside and entered the rich cave to fill their several sacks. They filled one sack, then another and still were far from satisfied.

By now the Demon's humour had turned to rage as he saw such greed. His smiled changed into a scowl. With a clap of thunder his great stone lips came crashing shut, locking the greedy brother and his wife firmly inside the mountain.

Early next morning, when the young brother ventured outside his house, he found the dog and cat and the two oxen carts standing empty. Nothing more.

Once again he uttered not a word. Yet as he glanced up, he felt quite certain that he saw the Demon of Stone Mountain give him a knowing wink.

Kotura, Lord of the Winds

In a Eskimo camp in the wilds of the far north lived an old man with his three daughters. The man was very poor. His choom—the deerskin tent that was home to his family—barely kept out the icy wind and driving snow. And when the frost was keen enough to singe their naked hands and faces, the three daughters could only huddle together round the fire for warmth. As they lay down to sleep at night, their father would rake through the ashes; then they would shiver throughout the long cold night 'til morning with no fire at all.

One day in the depths of winter, a snow-storm blew up and raged across the tundra. It whipped through the camp the first day, then the second, and on into the third. There seemed no end to the driving snow and fierce wind. No hunter, however bold, dared show his face outside his tent and families sat fearful in their chooms, hungry and cold, dreading that the camp would be blown clean away.

The old man and his daughters crouched in their tent harking to the howling of the blizzard.

The father said, 'If the storm continues for much longer, we shall all die for certain. It was sent by Kotura, Lord of the Winds. He must be very angry with us. There's only one way to appease him and save the camp: we must send him a wife from our clan. You, my eldest daughter, must go to Kotura and beg him to halt the blizzard.'

'But how am I to go?' asked the girl in alarm. 'I do not know the way.'

'I shall give you a sled,' said her father. 'Turn your face into the north wind, push the sled forward and follow wherever it leads. The wind will tear open the strings that bind your coat; yet you must not stop to tie them. The snow will fill your shoes; yet you must not stop to shake it out. Continue on your way until you arrive at a steep hill. When you have climbed to the top, only then may you halt to shake the snow from your shoes and do up your coat.

'Presently, a little bird will perch on your shoulder. Do not brush him away, be kind and caress him gently. Then jump on to your sled and let it run down the other side of the hill. It will take you straight to the door of Kotura's choom. Enter and touch nothing; just sit patiently and wait until he comes.'

Eldest daughter put on her coat, pointed the sled into the north wind and sent it gliding along before her.

She followed on foot and after a while the strings on her coat came undone, the swirling snow squeezed into her shoes and she was very, very cold. She did not heed her father's words: she stopped and began to tie the strings on her coat and shake the snow from her shoes. That done, she moved on.

On and on through the snow she went until at last she came to a steep hill. And when she finally reached the top, a little bird flew down and would have alighted on her shoulder had she not impatiently waved her hands to shoo him away. Alarmed, the bird fluttered up and circled above her three times before flying off.

Eldest daughter sat on her sled and rode down the hillside until she arrived at a giant choom. Straightaway she entered and glanced about her. The first thing that met her gaze was a fat piece of roast venison. Being hungry from her journey, she made a fire, warmed herself and tore off pieces of fat from the meat. She tore off one piece and ate it, then tore off another and ate that too, and another until she had eaten her fill. Just as all the fat was eaten she heard a noise behind her and a handsome young giant entered. It was Kotura himself.

He gazed at eldest daughter and said in his booming voice, 'Where are you from, girl? What is your mission here?'

'My father sent me,' replied the girl, 'to be your wife.'

Kotura frowned, fell silent, then finally said, 'I've brought home some meat from hunting. Set to work and cook it for me.'

Eldest daughter did as he said, and when the meat was cooked, Kotura bade her divide it into two parts.

'You and I will eat one part,' he said. 'The remainder you will take to my neighbour. But heed my words well: do not go into her choom. Wait outside until an old woman appears. Give her the meat and wait for her to return the empty dish.'

Eldest daughter took the meat and went out into the dark night. The wind was howling and the blizzard raging so wildly she could hardly see a thing before her. She struggled on a little way, then came to a halt and tossed the meat into the snow. That done, she returned to Kotura with the empty dish.

The giant looked at her sternly and said, 'Have you done as I said?'

'Certainly,' replied the girl.

'Then show me the dish, I wish to see what she gave you in return,' he said.

Eldest daughter showed him the empty dish. Kotura was silent. He ate his share of the meat hurriedly and lay down to sleep. At first light, he rose and brought some untanned deer hides into the tent.

'While I hunt,' he said, 'I want you to clean these hides and make me a coat, shoes and mittens from them. I shall try them on when I get back and judge whether

you are as clever with your hands as you are with your tongue.'

With those words, Kotura went off into the tundra. And eldest daughter set to work. By and by a wizened old woman covered in snow came into the tent.

'I have something in my eye, child,' she said. 'Please remove it for me.'

'I've no time. I'm too busy,' answered eldest daughter.

The old snow woman said nothing, turned away and left the tent. Eldest daughter was left alone. She cleaned the hides hastily and began cutting them roughly with a knife, hurrying to get her tasks done by nightfall. Indeed, in such a rush was she, that she did not even try to shape the garments properly, she was intent only on finishing her work as quickly as possible.

Late that evening, the young giant, Lord of the Winds, returned.

'Are my clothes ready?' he asked at once.

'They are,' eldest daughter replied.

Kotura took the garments one by one, and ran his hands carefully over them: the hides were rough to the touch so badly were they cleaned, so poorly were they cut, so carelessly were they sewn together. And they were altogether too small for him.

At that he flew into a fearful rage, picked up eldest daughter and flung her far, far into the dark night. She landed in a deep snowdrift and soon froze to death.

The howling of the wind became even fiercer.

Back in the nomad camp, the old father sat in his choom and harkened to the bitterness of the northern winds.

Finally, in deep despair, he said to his two remaining daughters, 'Eldest daughter did not heed my words, I fear. That is why the wind is still shrieking and roaring its anger. Kotura is in a terrible temper. You must go to him, second daughter.'

The old man made a sled, told the girl just what he had said to the one before, and sent her on her way. The lonely choom became misty with the warm tears of its last two occupants, the father and his youngest daughter.

Meanwhile, second daughter pointed the sled into the north wind and, giving it a push, walked along behind it. The strings of her coat came undone and the snow forced its way into her shoes. Soon she was numb with cold and,

heedless of her father's warning, she shook the snow from her shoes and tied the strings of her coat sooner than she was instructed.

She came to the steep hill and climbed to the top. There, seeing the little bird fluttering towards her, she waved her hands crossly and shooed him away. Then quickly she climbed into her sled and rode down the hillside straight to Kotura's choom. She entered the tent, made a fire, ate her fill of the roast venison and lay down to sleep.

When Kotura returned, he was surprised to find the girl asleep on his bed. The roar of his deep voice woke her at once and she explained that her father had sent her to be his wife.

Kotura frowned, fell silent, then shouted at her gruffly, 'Then why do you lie there sleeping? I am hungry, be quick and prepare some meat.'

As soon as the meat was ready, Kotura ordered second daughter to take it from the pot and cut it in half.

'You and I will eat one half,' he said. 'And you will take the other to my neighbour. But do not enter her choom: wait outside for the dish to be returned.'

Second daughter took the meat and went outside into the blinding storm. The wind was howling so hard and the black night was so smothering that she could see and hear nothing at all. So, fearing to take another step, she tossed the meat as far as she could and returned to Kotura's tent.

'Have you given the meat to my neighbour?' he asked.

'Of course I have,' replied second daughter.

'You haven't been long,' he said. 'Show me the dish, I want to see what she gave you in return.'

Somewhat afraid, second daughter did as she was bid, and Kotura frowned as he saw the empty dish. But he said not a word and went to bed. In the morning, he brought in some untanned hides and told second daughter to make him a coat, shoes and mittens by nightfall.

'Set to work,' he said. 'This evening I shall judge your handiwork.'

With those words, Kotura went off and second daughter got down to her task. She was in a great hurry, knowing that she must complete the job by nightfall. By and by, a wizened old woman covered in snow came into the tent. She spoke to second daughter.

'I've something in my eye, child,' she said. 'Pray help
me to take it out; I cannot manage it by myself.'

'Oh, go away and don't bother me,' said the girl. 'I am
too busy to leave my work.'

The snow woman went away without a word.

As darkness came, Kotura returned from hunting.

'Are my new clothes ready?' he asked.

'Here they are,' replied second daughter.

He tried on the garments and saw at once they were
poorly cut and much too small. Flying into a rage, he
flung second daughter even farther than her sister. And
she too met a cold death in the snow.

Back home the old father sat in his choom with his
youngest daughter, waiting in vain for the storm to
abate. But the blizzard redoubled its force, and it seemed
the camp would be blown away at any minute.

'My daughters did not heed my words,' the old man
reflected sadly. 'They have angered Kotura even more.
Go to him, my last daughter, though it breaks my heart
to lose you; you alone can now save our clan from certain
doom.'

Youngest daughter left the camp, turned her face into

the north wind and pushed the sled before her. The wind
shrieked and seethed about her. The snowflakes powdered her red-rimmed eyes all but blinding her. Yet she
somehow staggered on through the blizzard mindful of
her father's every word. The strings of her coat came
undone—but she did not stop to tie them. The snow
forced its way into her shoes—but she did not stop to
shake it out. And, although her face was numb and her
lungs were almost bursting, she did not pause for breath.
Only when she had reached the hilltop did she halt to
shake out the snow from her shoes and tie the strings of
her coat.

Just at that moment, a little bird flew down and
perched on her shoulder. Instead of chasing him away,
she gently stroked his downy breast.

When the bird flew away, she sat upon her sled and
glided over the snow, down the hillside, right to Kotura's
door.

Without showing her fear, the young girl went boldly
into the tent and sat down patiently waiting for the giant
to appear. It was not long before the doorflap was lifted
and in came the handsome young giant, Lord of the
Winds.

When he set eyes on the young girl, a smile lit up his

solemn face. 'Why have you come to me?' he asked.

'My father sent me to ask you to calm the storm,' she said quietly. 'For if you do not, all our people will die.'

Kotura frowned and said gruffly, 'Make up the fire and cook some meat. I am hungry and so must you be too, for I see you have touched nothing since you arrived.'

Youngest daughter prepared the meat, took it from the pot and handed it to Kotura in a dish. But he instructed her to take half to his neighbour.

Obediently, youngest daghter took the dish of meat and went outside into the snowstorm. Where was she to go? Where was the neighbour's choom to be found in this wilderness?

Then suddenly, from out of nowhere, a little bird flew before her face—that selfsame bird she had caressed on the hillside. Now it flew before her, as if beckoning her on. Whichever way the bird flew, there she followed. At last she could make out a wisp of smoke spiralling upwards and mingling with the swirling snowflakes.

Youngest daughter was very relieved as she made for the smoke, thinking the choom must be there. Yet as she drew near, she saw to her surprise that the smoke was coming from a mound of snow; no choom was to be seen!

She walked round and round the mound of snow and prodded it with her foot. Straightaway a door appeared before her and an old, old woman poked her head out.

'Who are you?' she screeched. 'And why have you come here?'

'I have brought you some meat, Grannie,' youngest daughter replied. 'Kotura asked me to bring it to you.'

'Kotura, you say?' said the old woman, chewing on a black pipe. 'Very well, then, wait here.'

Youngest daughter waited by the strange igloo and at last the old woman reappeared and handed her back the wooden dish. There was something in the dish, but the girl could not make it out in the dark. With a word of thanks, she took the dish and returned to Kotura.

'Why were you so long?' Kotura asked. 'Did you find the snow woman's home?'

'Yes, I did, but it was a long way,' she replied.

'Give me the dish that I might see what she has given you,' said the giant.

When he looked into the dish he saw that it contained

two sharp knives and some bone needles and scrapers for dressing hides.

The giant chuckled and said, 'You have some fine gifts to keep you busy.'

At dawn Kotura rose and brought some deerskins into the choom. As before, he gave orders that new shoes, mittens and a coat were to be made by nightfall.

'Should you make them well,' he said, 'you shall be my wife.'

As soon as Kotura had gone, youngest daughter set to work. The snow woman's gifts indeed proved very useful: there was all she needed to make the garments.

But how could she do it in a single day? That was impossible!

All the same, she carefully dressed and scraped the skins, cut and sewed so quickly that her fingers were soon raw and bleeding.

As she was about her work, the doorflap was raised

142

and in came the old snow woman.

'Help me, my child,' she said. 'There's a mote in my eye. Pray help me to take it out.'

At once youngest daughter set aside her work and soon had the mote out of the old woman's eye.

'That's better,' said the snow woman, 'my eye does not hurt any more. Now, child, look into my right ear and see what you can see.'

Youngest daughter looked into the old woman's right ear and gasped in surprise.

'What do you see?' the snow woman asked.

'I see a maid sitting in your ear,' the girl replied.

'Then, why don't you call to her? She will help you make Kotura's clothes.'

At her call, not one but four maids jumped from the snow woman's ear and immediately set to work. They dressed the skins, scraped them smooth, cut and sewed them into shape, and very soon the garments were all ready. Then the snow woman took the four maids back into her ear and left the choom.

As darkness fell, Kotura returned.

'Have you completed your tasks?' he asked.

'Yes, I have,' the girl said.

'Then show me the new clothes so that I may try them on.'

Youngest daughter handed him the clothes, and Kotura passed his great hand gently over them. The skins were soft and supple to the touch. He put them on—the coat and the shoes and the mittens. And they were neither small nor large. They fitted him perfectly.

Kotura smiled. 'I like you, youngest daughter,' he said. 'And my mother and four sisters like you, too. You work well, and you have much courage. You braved a terrible storm so that your people might not die. And you did all that you were told. Pray stay with me and be my wife.'

No sooner had the words passed his lips than the storm in the tundra was stilled. No longer did the Eskimo people hide from the north wind in their tents. They were saved. One by one they emerged into the bright sunshine.

And with them came the old father, tears of joy glistening on his sunken cheeks, proud that his youngest, dearest daughter had saved the people from the blizzard.

143

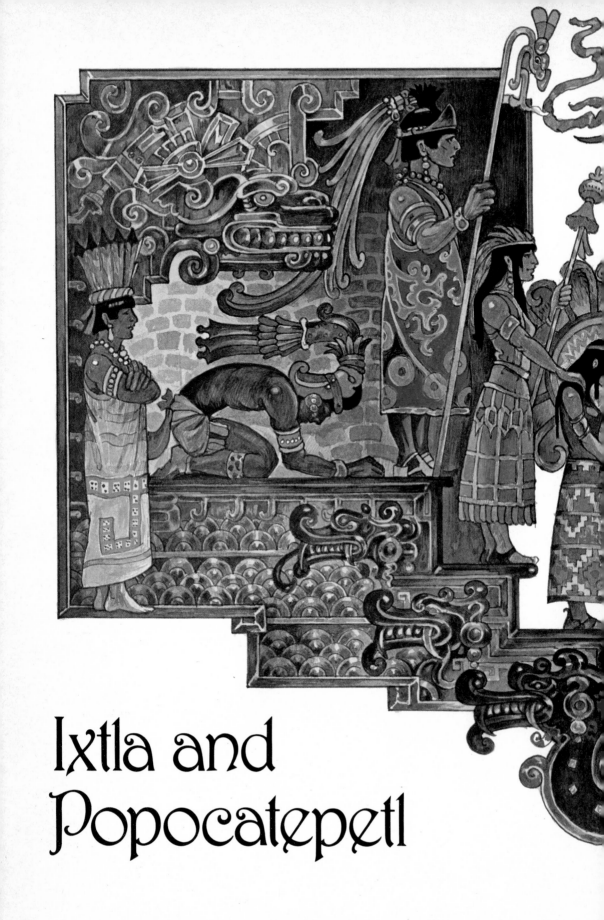

Ixtla and Popocatepetl

There was once an emperor in the ancient Aztec city of Tenochtitlan, in what is now the great valley of Mexico, who was very powerful. Some thought him wise, others were more sparing in their praise. But the emperor ruled firmly and with much splendour, keeping out the fierce tribes that lived beyond the mountains.

When the emperor was in his middle years, the empress bore him an heir to his rich throne. The baby, being a fair and bonny girl, was given the name Ixtla. The emperor and empress loved her very much and, since she was their only child, prepared her as she grew to rule after their death.

Being a kind and pretty girl, Ixtla was never short of

friends, and when she was older it was no surprise that she should fall in love. Whereas for most girls that would have been a joyful event, for poor Ixtla it could never be. Her father, trusting no one, wanted her to reign alone when he died; so he had forbidden her to marry.

Ixtla's beloved was a warrior in the service of her father, a strong, handsome youth named Popocatepetl. He and Ixtla loved each other more than words can tell, and though they were happy just to be together, they knew that true joy could not be theirs unless they could marry and have children of their own. Despite their pleas, the emperor would not be swayed: Ixtla must never wed.

When the emperor was already old, he fell gravely ill. It was at that fateful moment that enemy tribes from beyond the mountains poured down upon his kingdom and attacked his subjects. Without wise counsel to guide them, the emperor's soldiers fell back before the onslaught, until all that remained of the once splendid empire was the city of Tenochtitlan.

The ailing emperor would not appoint a general to lead his men into battle because he would not trust anyone sufficiently. Yet he knew full well that unless he made a bold decision soon there would be no empire for him or his daughter to rule. Thus, he made a pronouncement: whoever succeeded in defeating the enemy armies would wed his daughter and rule with her over the entire empire.

Ixtla was much afraid when she heard her father's proclamation. She feared that some other bold warrior, not her beloved Popocatepetl, would find a way of defeating the hostile tribes. She knew she would rather die than marry any other.

The soldiers, of course, received new heart when they heard the news. To marry the beautiful princess and rule the empire was a prize indeed. Each soldier fought three times as fiercely as before and with three times more guile. Never were there more courageous warriors on the field of battle.

Yet the war was long and hard. By now the fierce tribes from beyond the mountains had entrenched themselves around Lake Texacoco before the walls of Tenochtitlan. Many a brave man perished, cut down by sharp obsidian machetes or pierced by spears and lances.

Many too were the soldiers who excelled in valour on the field of battle.

However, there was one warrior who fought twice as valiantly as all the others and survived. It was Popocatepetl, the only love of the fair Ixtla. Finally, it was he, protected by his thick quilted cloak soaked in brine, who led the mighty thrust forward that routed the enemy armies and drove them from the valley. With much rejoicing, all the soldiers on the battlefield acclaimed Popocatepetl as their leader. After a welcome night's rest from their exertions, they set off to bring these happy tidings to the emperor.

Yet there were some evil soldiers who were jealous of Popocatepetl. Without resting for the night, they slipped away and by dawn were standing before the emperor in his palace. And the news they bore was, that although the emperor's army had won the war, their leader Popocatepetl had fallen in battle.

When the emperor heard the news, he at once demanded that the hero's body should be brought before him so that he might arrange a proper funeral. But the evil soldiers said that Popocatepetl had been slain on the banks of Lake Texacoco and fallen into the water.

Soon these false tidings reached the ears of the Princess Ixtla. Nothing her father or mother could do or say was solace to her in her great grief. She wept and wept, would not eat or drink, and nothing the best healers in the city could do could save her. She did not wish to live without her beloved Popocatepetl, and in no time at all breathed her last breath.

It was just as she lay dying that the victorious procession with Popocatepetl at its head reached the gates of the city. The conquering soldiers marched through the streets to great cheering from the crowds and made their way to the emperor's grand palace. In triumph, Popocatepetl announced before the emperor the news of the great victory. With tears of joy upon his cheeks, he claimed the princess's hand in marriage.

The emperor bowed his head in grief. He told the bold warrior how he had been misinformed, how his daughter had fallen ill at the false news of Popocatepetl's death and how she had died just before his arrival.

In an instant, the young man's flushed countenance turned ashen; taking his trusty sword he sought out those

147

false prophets of his doom and challenged each one in single combat. In the presence of the emperor and all the other victorious soldiers, he fought his duels and killed each and every one of the jealous men. No one tried to stop him.

That task accomplished, he made for the palace chamber where Ixtla's body lay in death's repose upon her couch. Gently, he lifted it up and bore it in his arms out of the palace and the city. No one dared to stop him.

When he had walked some distance from the city, he halted and gestured to the warriors who had followed in his wake. He instructed them to build a giant pyramid out of all the stones and rocks that lay upon the plain. The men toiled hard and fast, while Popocatepetl stood before them holding the dead body of the princess in his arms. By sunset the mighty edifice was complete. It rose up sheer and white, dazzling in the sun's dying rays.

Slowly, Popocatepetl climbed alone, still bearing his loved one's body with him. At the summit, he gently laid the body of Ixtla, the princess he loved so dearly, on a golden bier.

That night he slept alongside the silent grave. Then with the first mists of dawn, he descended to the faithful warriors.

'Now build another pyramid close by,' he said, 'just higher than the first, that I might look down upon my beloved's grave.'

In the purple haze of evening, the second great pyramid was ready and Popocatepetl began his lonely ascent of the great mountain of stone, this time bearing with him a flaming pinewood torch. When he reached the summit, the warriors below could see the ash-grey smoke and the bright red flame lighting up the dark night sky. Slowly, the smoke turned mauve, then deep scarlet, the colour of blood.

Popocatepetl stood there, tall and proud, holding his flaming torch in memory of the fair Ixtla who had died of her love for him.

The snows came, the years passed, the man-made pyramids of stone turned to white-capped mountains. And they stand there still. The one to the north of Tenochtitlan is known as Ixtla, the Fair Maiden; the one to the south, just higher and still smoking, is known as Popocatepetl, the Smoky Mountain.

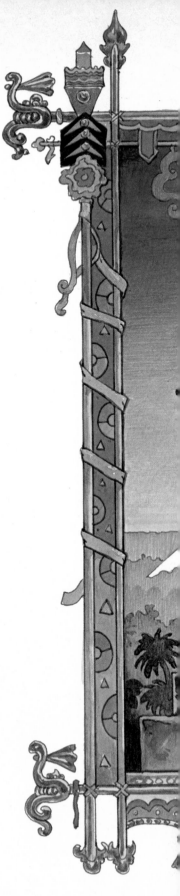

The Ugly Girl

In the days before the Mahdi's rule, there lived a poor man in the Sudan who had as many sons as he had fingers.

'A veritable handful of happiness, Subhan Allah— Glory be to Allah,' he would tell his friends.

For the sons could help him till the land, sow seeds and harvest the crops.

'A girl is as a stone in the mother's belly,' he would say, hoping his wife would bear him plenty more sons.

But his wife was of a different mind. A son was fine for helping in the fields, but not for helping her in the home. She wanted a daughter.

'Who will lay out my body when the time comes?' she asked her husband. 'Who will close the eyes that see death, dress the corpse and arrange the limbs? That is no work for a son.'

They could not agree. So one night the poor man's wife stole away to consult a holy fakir.

'Though I am very poor,' the woman said to the fakir, 'I will give you the first calf of the season, if you make my next born a daughter.'

The fakir closed his eyes and softly asked the woman's name, her mother's name and that of her grandmother too. For some moments he sat quite still, cross-legged, then rose and picked up a large bowl filled with camel's milk. Over this he drew some signs and mumbled several spells in communion with the holy spirits. That done he opened wide his staring eyes and, taking a bottle, filled it to the brim with the camel's milk.

'Wait until the moon is new,' he told the poor woman, 'then wash yourself with this milk for seven nights. Allah be willing, a daughter shall be born to you.'

The woman took the bottle eagerly, offered many thanks and did exactly as instructed. When the moon was new she washed herself all over with the camel's milk for seven nights. Thus it happened, in the passing of the days, her belly began to swell and, when the fateful day arrived, she gave birth to a daughter.

The wife was overjoyed. For several days she fasted and gave up thanks in prayer, asking the holy spirits above and on the earth to guard her daughter and bring her joy. Her husband too, on seeing the little baby, grew mighty fond of her. He refrained from eating and drinking for four full days, granted small alms to those even poorer than himself, and offered prayers in thanksgiving to Allah the Almighty.

Their many relatives and friends, on hearing of the news, came from far and near to add their felicitations. 'Mabrook. Mabrook,' they all said in congratulation.

So it was that the daughter grew up in love and happiness. Yet, sad to tell, a dark cloud cast a shadow over her advancing years: the older she became, the uglier she grew. So unpleasant were her looks that her despairing mother, fearing lest the girl be driven to distraction by her own reflection, cast out all mirrors from the home and forbade any visitor to bring one in.

Despite her unkind features, the young girl was as gentle and modest as she was ugly. Her good nature endeared her to everyone she met, and she had many friends. All the same, when she was fully grown, no man came to court her or look upon her as his desired wife. So unattractive was she that, as the years passed on, her parents wondered whether anyone would ever wish to wed their daughter.

The mother paid several visits to the holy fakirs, but none could help. Then one day, to the astonishment of all, the girl's own cousin, a young and handsome man with a rich fortune of his own, arrived to ask the parents for their daughter's hand. Everyone was overjoyed.

As was the custom, the wedding celebrations commenced forty days before the marriage, and all the

friends and relatives arrived to wish long life and many
children to the happy pair. But though they all repeated
the customary 'Mabrook. Mabrook,' their faces showed
what they were thinking. Why should such a handsome
man select such an ugly maiden for his wife? There were
surely enough beautiful girls in the land.

The young girl did not notice anything amiss. After
all, she told herself, it was the custom to seek a bride
among one's kinsfolk before one chose a stranger. So
she joined in the celebrations in her innocence, never
thinking, as the others did, of how very lucky she was.

There was one girl in the company whose heart was
heavy with grief and envy; she herself had long loved the
handsome cousin, and though she was the ugly girl's best
friend, she felt that she was more suited to marry him.
For she was rich and beautiful, a glittering gem beside
the poor, ugly girl. When she first heard of the proposed
betrothal, she laughed unkindly saying, 'Just wait until
he's seen her face, he'll change his mind at once.'

But she was wrong. The poor girl's looks seemed to
make no difference; indeed, the handsome suitor
appeared not to notice them at all. So when the rich girl
realised she had lost him to her ugly friend, she began to
hatch a cruel plan. She went to her friend and asked her
innocently, 'My dearest, nearest friend, tell me, have you
ever seen your face?'

The girl gazed at her with startled eyes. 'Why no,' she
answered frankly. 'Come to think of it, I have not.'

'Then you should,' the spiteful girl said, and turned
around and left.

As soon as her friend had departed, the ugly girl began
to wonder how she really looked. For the words had
planted a seed in her mind that now began to grow and
grow. She went to her mother and asked for a mirror to
look at her reflection.

'Why should you see your face before your wedding?'
her poor mother said in desperation. 'It could bring you
both bad luck.'

Yet the more the mother tried to turn her mind against
it, the more the girl desired to see her features. She bided
her time until the sun had set; then, in the clear light of
the moon, she crept out into the night and made her way
down to the river.

The bright moon was in its fourteenth night and shone

down upon the smooth waters of the river like fire on burnished gold. With fast-beating heart, the girl waded into the cool waters and when the river came above her knees she bent down to look into the water. For the first time in her life she saw her ugly face.

So utterly miserable was she that her only thought was to end her life at once. 'Nobody must see my ugly face again,' she cried. But she could not drown herself in the river, because, she thought, people might come and stare at her dead face, and whisper about her ugliness.

No, she would walk out into the desert and die there alone when she was far from any habitation. The vultures would come and peck her flesh and nothing would be left but sun-bleached bones. So, crying bitterly, she set off into the desert.

She had not gone far when suddenly she heard a voice behind her say softly, 'Maiden, what is your errand at so late an hour?'

In fear, she drew her veil quickly across her face before glancing round. She was surprised to see a beautiful girl in rich, strange clothes walking behind her. The beautiful girl smiled so kindly, however, that the ugly girl's fear soon faded. After more gentle words from her companion, the ugly girl unburdened her heavy heart and told her story and her intent.

'My cousin obviously took pity on me because no one else would have me,' she said. 'He is so rich and handsome, while I am poor and ugly. I must kill myself to set him free from his promise. There is no other way.'

'Look at me,' the stranger said gently. 'Am I not beautiful? Would you say that your cousin would wish to marry me?'

The girl looked sadly at the flower-like face.

'You are very beautiful,' she said. 'Of that there is no doubt. Many men would surely wish to marry you.'

'That then is how you appear before your cousin,' the stranger said. 'For I am, in truth, your Good Nature. I am with you all the time, night and day. It is the beauty of the heart that makes a person truly handsome. So go back home and live your life in joy and confidence.'

Thereupon the stranger vanished into the night.

The girl returned home and quietly went to bed. A few days later she and her cousin were wed, and lived together in trust and love for the remainder of their lives.

The King of the Cats

Down in the west of England, not far from the pleasant
town of Frome, there stood a sexton's cottage alongside
the village church. For all I know it stands there still, and
the graveyard too, which holds the crumbling bones of
many generations of Somerset folk.

About two centuries ago, one autumn evening in
between daylight and dusk, Jack Luscombe the grave-
digger was sitting by an open grave, having a rest. He sat
there enjoying the last few pulls on his old clay pipe
before going home. Another day gone. Jack had made a
start on old Mr Fordyce's grave, and was fair content

with what he'd done. Another few feet tomorrow and they could have themselves a rare old funeral on Saturday with lots of flowers and lots of weeping.

Suddenly, old Jack heard a noise that turned his stomach over, and made him feel quite queer. It was like a crowd of cats miaowing, but in an odd, low chorus, as if the church organ had bust its bellows yet again.

To be sure it wasn't Tom, Jack's old black cat. He'd be back home snoozing, stretched out on the rug before the fire, nice and cosy. A right lazy devil he was, but a rum old fellow all the same. He was silky black all over save for a white patch on his chest and he had strange almond-shaped eyes and damson-coloured ears. He liked his comforts did old Tom and would not be in the graveyard at this late hour.

Jack Luscombe peered into the gloom across the gaunt, grey tombstones, and saw a sight that made him rub his eyes in disbelief. Coming towards him were nine silky black cats bearing a coffin all draped in black and on the very top of the velvet pall lay a small gold coronet.

The grave-digger held his breath, not daring even to puff at his pipe or let his whiskers twitch. The procession was heading straight towards him. At every third step, those nine black pall-bearers let out a low miaow in chorus, just like the wind howling through the yew trees.

As they came nearer, Jack could see them more distinctly. Their eyes shone through the gathering gloom with a strange amber light. Eight of them bore the coffin, while the biggest, blackest beast walked ahead, for all the world as if he were leading a group of mourners. They moved softly and solemnly between the shadowy tombstones, never stumbling, never stepping on a grave.

Poor old Jack. His knees were knocking, his white hair stood on end and he mumbled whatever hasty prayers he could recall. Yet still the cats came on until they reached the far side of Mr Fordyce's half-dug grave. Then they stopped.

Those nine black cats stood still, waiting, staring, looking straight at Jack, twitching their damson-coloured ears. No one said a word. At last, the biggest, blackest cat stepped round the grave and addressed Jack in a human voice and these are the very words he said:

'Tell Tom Tildrum Tim Toldrum's dead.'

No more no less. As clear as the church bell.

That was enough for Jack. He was up and away, running for dear life before those cats could pounce on him. He reached his house all out of breath, burst through the door and bolted it fast behind him. He startled his poor wife out of her wits.

'What's put the wind up you, Jack Luscombe?' she asked, staring at her husband's ashen face.

As soon as he could speak, Jack exclaimed, 'Who's Tom Tildrum, that's what I'd like to know!'

His wife and cat both started up together.

'How should I know?' said his wife. 'Why do you want this Tommy Tildrum fellow? What on earth's the matter with you?'

'Oh, you'd never believe it,' said her husband. 'I've seen such odd sights in the graveyard tonight, over by Mr Fordyce's grave.'

He fell into his old armchair and began to recount the tale of his adventures. Now and then he had to stop to get his breath back, leaning his head against the chair and closing his red-rimmed eyes. Each time he did so, his old black cat would let out a growl or groan or grating noise as if impatient to hear the story's end. A queer gleam had come into his almond-shaped eyes as he stared up at the storyteller.

'Well I never,' said old Jack. 'You'd think that cat knew what I was saying by the look he's giving me.'

'Go on with you,' his wife replied. 'Let's hear the end of this daft story.'

'Well now,' continued Jack, 'that big black cat with saucer eyes comes up and says to me—that's right, my dear, he spoke to me in a human voice. He says, "Tell Tom Tildrum Tim Toldrum's dead." As true as I sit here now.'

Jack had had enough scares for one night, but now he had another. For as he was talking, the old tom-cat had raised himself right up, arched his back and stood there staring, his black tail erect, his damson-coloured ears alert. Then he opened up his mouth and spoke. 'Why, I be jiggered! Fancy, old Tim's dead! Then I be King of the Cats!'

Before the grave-digger and his wife could move, old Tom had sprung up the chimney and disappeared in a pall of soot.

He was never seen again.

Rip Van Winkle

At the foot of the Catskill Mountains west of the Hudson River, where the purple-blue of the hills melt away into the fresh green of the valley, lies a village of great antiquity. It was founded by Dutch colonists in the early times of American history, just about when the good Peter Stuyvesant ruled the province, which in those days was still a British colony.

In that same village, in one of the houses built of small yellow bricks brought from Holland, with latticed windows and gable fronts and a weathercock on the roof, there lived a simple, good-natured fellow by the name of Rip Van Winkle. Truth to tell, his house was sadly time-worn and weather-beaten. For Rip was one of those men who was ever ready to attend to anybody's business but his own. He would never refuse to assist a neighbour in the roughest work yet he found it impossible to keep his own house and farm in order.

The children of the village would shout with joy whenever they saw him coming. He would tell them exciting stories of ghosts and witches and Red Indians, teach them to fly kites and play marbles, and make them toys. Thus, whenever he walked through the village he would have a crowd of children clambering on his back and playing a thousand tricks on him. Even the dogs would never bark at him, but run and lick his hand.

His own children were as ragged and unruly as if they belonged to nobody in particular. His first son Rip, an urchin the spitting image of his father, looked like inheriting his father's amiable habits along with his old clothes.

The bane of Rip Van Winkle's life was Dame Van Winkle. When he had married her she was as sweet-tempered as all maids are upon their wedding day. But

160

once she'd got him home that shy tongue and gentle smile turned sour, and a tart temper took their place. Times grew worse with Rip as the years of wedded bliss rolled on. You know what they say: a sharp tongue is the only tool that grows sharper with constant use.

Rip's boon companion was his dog Wolf, who was as hen-pecked as his master. For Dame Van Winkle looked on them both with the same vinegar eye, regarding them as companions in laziness, one leading the other astray. Wolf was as spirited as his master until he crossed the threshold of the house, then his tail dropped to the floor, or trailed between his legs, and he would creep along with many a sidelong glance at the mistress. The smallest waving of a broomstick or a ladle would send him yelping to the door or under the table.

Poor Rip's one escape from the mounting toils of his farm and the nagging of his wife was to creep away, gun in hand and Wolf at his side, into the forest. Not that the idle, good-natured pair of hunters would ever catch a bird or rabbit, but they could sit and doze in the sun.

On one such blissful day in autumn, Rip wandered with Wolf into one of the highest parts of the Catskill Mountains. Late in the afternoon, he lay down to rest on a green knoll that crowned the brow of a hill. From an opening between the trees he could overlook the country below for many a mile. He spied in the distance the mighty Hudson moving on its majestic course into the

blue highlands. On the other side of the hill he looked down into a deep glen, wild, lonely and scarcely lit by the rays of the setting sun.

For some time Rip lay there musing, sharing the contents of his knapsack with Wolf who, in turn, was staring thoughtfully at the lengthening blue shadows of evening. Rip realised with a sigh that it would be dark long before he reached the village, and he knew full well the terrible scolding he could expect from Dame Van Winkle. He stood up to go and was on his way down the mountain when he heard a voice from the distance calling his name.

'Hallooo. Halloo. Rip Van Winkle. Rip Van Winkle.'

He glanced around, yet saw nothing but a black crow winging its solitary way across the mountain peaks. He thought his imagination must be playing tricks with him, and he turned again to descend. Suddenly, he heard the same cry ring through the still night air.

'Hallooo. Halloo. Rip Van Winkle, Rip Van Winkle.'

This time the hair on Wolf's back bristled and he gave a low growl.

Rip now felt a vague anxiety stealing over him. He looked fearfully down into the glen and saw a strange figure slowly climbing up the rocks, bending low under the weight of something he carried on his back. Rip was surprised to see any human soul in this lonely, godforsaken place, but fancying it to be a neighbour in need of his assistance, he hastened down to give a hand.

As he came nearer, he was still more astonished at the fellow's odd appearance. He was a short, squarely-built man with thick brown hair and grizzled beard. His clothes were of an old-fashioned Dutch variety: a cloth jerkin belted round the waist and two or three pairs of breeches, the top one decorated with rows of buttons down the sides, and bunched at the knees. On his shoulder he was carrying a stout keg of what seemed to be liquor. He was gesturing to Rip to help him with the load.

Though rather taken aback at this strange sight, Rip came forward to lend a hand, and the two of them clambered together up a narrow gully, evidently the dry bed of some old mountain stream. As they climbed upwards, Rip every now and then heard long, rolling peals like distant thunder; it seemed to come from the

deep ravine to which their rugged path was leading. Passing through the ravine they emerged into a hollow, roofless hall inside the mountain. Its walls were sheer up to the top, over which hung the branches of trees reaching out despairingly into the void, allowing only brief glimpses of the azure sky and bright evening cloud.

During the whole ascent Rip and his companion had climbed in silence. While Rip had wondered greatly why a keg of liquor should be carried up this wild mountain, there was something awe-inspiring about the man that stilled his tongue.

On entering the hollow hall, Rip received a further shock. For there, on a level platform of stone in the very centre, was a group of odd-looking men playing at skittles. They were dressed in a quaint, outmoded

fashion, just like his companion. Some wore short doublets, others linen jerkins with long knives stuck in their belts, and most wore enormous baggy breeches, like the guide's.

Their faces too were most uncommon: one had a large straggly beard, broad ruddy face and small piggy eyes; the face of another seemed to consist entirely of nose and was topped by a large white sugar-loaf hat set off with a red cock's tail feather. All the men had long beards of various shapes and colours.

One man seemed to be their chief. He was a stout old gentleman with a weather-beaten look, a laced doublet, high-crowned hat with feather, red stockings and high-heeled boots with roses on them. The whole company reminded Rip of the figures in the old Flemish painting which hung in the parlour of the village pub; it had been brought over from Holland at the time the Dutch first settled in America.

What was even more odd about this company was that the men were the most melancholy group of sportsmen Rip had ever encountered. The skittlers maintained the gravest of faces and no one uttered a word. Nothing interrupted the stillness of the scene but the noise of the skittles which, as they fell, echoed round the mountain walls like rumbling peals of thunder.

As Rip approached, the men suddenly set aside their play, and stared at him with such fixed, harsh eyes that his heart turned over and his knees knocked together. His guide now emptied the contents of the stout keg into several flagons and made signs to Rip to pour drinks out for the assembled company. He did so in fear and trembling. The men drank the liquor in an eerie silence and then went back to their game.

Bit by bit Rip's awe and fear subsided. He even made so bold, when no eye was on him, to taste the liquor, which struck him as an excellent brew—a dark mellow ale such as he'd never tried before. Rip was naturally a thirsty soul and he repeated his visits to the flagon so often that it was not long before his eyes were swimming in his head. At last, he fell into a deep, helpless slumber.

On waking he found himself on that same green knoll from where he had first seen the old man with the keg. He rubbed his eyes and saw it was a bright and sunny morning. The birds were twittering among the bushes and the eagle wheeled elegantly aloft breasting the early morning breeze.

Rip thought he must have slept all night. He recalled the happenings before he fell asleep: the odd fellow with the keg of liquor, the mountain ravine, the hollow hall inside the cliffs, the silent game of skittles and the flagon of ale. . . .

'Oh dear, oh dear, that strong ale!' thought Rip. 'What on earth am I going to tell Dame Van Winkle?'

He looked round for his gun, but saw nothing save an old rusty firepiece lying by him, the lock hanging off, the wooden butt all worm-eaten and rotten. Of course, he suspected that those strange skittlers had played a trick on him and robbed him of his gun. Wolf too had

disappeared; he'd probably gone running after a squirrel or partridge. Rip whistled for his dog and shouted but no Wolf was to be seen.

He was more than a little cross by now and made up his mind to return to the scene of last night's party and demand his dog and gun. Yet as he rose to walk off, he found himself stiff in the joints and by no means as sprightly as he normally was.

'This damp mountain grass will lay me up with a fit of

rheumatism, I'll be darned,' thought Rip. 'Then I'll catch it from Dame Van Winkle.'

Somehow he climbed down into the glen and found the gully up which he and his companion had clambered the previous evening. But to his astonishment a mountain stream was now cascading down it and filling the glen with rushing noises. He worked his weary way along its sides until at length he reached the spot where the ravine had opened through the cliffs into the hollow hall. But no traces of the opening remained. The rocks towered high and sheer before him in an impenetrable wall. Over its summit the torrent came tumbling down in a white sheet of foaming water into the black basin below.

Poor Rip, bewildered, could go no farther. He again called and whistled after his dog. But he was only answered by the cawing of a flock of idle crows who seemed to scoff at his desperation. What was he to do? The morning was getting on and he was famished for want of breakfast. It was sad about his dog and gun and he was even sadder at the thought of what his wife would say. But he could not stay there forever in the mountains. He shook his puzzled head, shouldered the rusty firepiece and turned his steps homeward with a heavy, troubled heart.

As he came near the village he passed a number of people but no one whom he recognised, which surprised him somewhat since he fancied he knew everyone in those parts. There was something too about their clothes that struck him as odd. They all stared back at him, looking as surprised at him as he was at them. He stopped, pushed back his broad hat and stroked his chin to puzzle it out. To his amazement he found his beard had grown a good foot long!

He had now reached the outskirts of the village. A band of strange children and dogs, none of whom he recognised, ran at his heels, the children making fun of his clothes. The very village had altered and grown bigger. There were rows of houses he had never seen before. Strange names hung above the doors, and there were strange faces at the windows—everything was different.

Could his mind be playing tricks with him? Surely this was his native village which he had left the day before? There stood the Catskill Mountains; there ran the

Hudson River in the distance; there was every fell and dale just as it had always been. Rip was even more puzzled.

'That strong ale last night has properly confused my head,' he muttered.

It was with some apprehension that he approached his own house, fearing at any moment to hear the shrill voice of Dame Van Winkle. He found the house all right, but completely in decay. The roof had fallen in, the windows were all broken, and the doors were hanging off the hinges. He passed through the broken door and found the house empty, forlorn and evidently abandoned. He called loudly for his wife and children and the faithful Wolf. The lonely rooms echoed for a moment with his voice, and then all was silent.

He now hastened to his old resort, the village inn where he had sat and smoked many a peaceful pipe and drunk not a few glasses of good ale. That too was gone. A

large wooden building stood in its place with a sign above the door, "The Union Hotel, Prop. Jonathan Doolittle." Gone too was the ruby face of good King George upon the hanging sign; instead there was a painting of a figure in a blue frock coat, cocked hat and sword in hand, with the legend "General Washington". From the very top of the inn fluttered a flag with stars and stripes upon a white-painted pole.

There was, as usual, a crowd of red-faced folk about the door, but none that Rip recognised. Where was old

Nicholas Vedder with his amiable face, his double chins and long black pipe? Or Van Bummel, the schoolmaster, reading out the contents of the newspaper? The very character of these people seemed changed: instead of the old drowsy, good-humoured atmosphere there was a bustling, argumentative tone about the place.

The sudden appearance of Rip, with his long, grizzled beard, his rough clothes and his rusty firepiece soon attracted the attention of the tavern regulars. They crowded round him, eyeing him from head to toe. They demanded to know what he wanted and where he had come from.

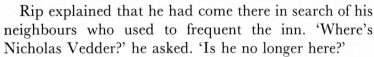

Rip explained that he had come there in search of his neighbours who used to frequent the inn. 'Where's Nicholas Vedder?' he asked. 'Is he no longer here?'

There was silence for a while, then an old man replied, 'Why, he's been dead and gone these eighteen years. There's a wooden board in the churchyard that marks his grave, though it's covered in weeds and overgrown with grass.'

'Where's Van Bummel the schoolmaster?' asked Rip.

'He went off to the wars, became a great general and is now in Congress,' said the same old man.

Rip's heart sank at hearing of these strange changes in his home and friends. Each answer puzzled him; there were so many things he could not understand. What wars? What was Congress?

He had no courage to ask after any more friends, but at last he cried out in despair, 'Does anybody here know Rip Van Winkle?'

'Oh, yes, Rip Van Winkle!' readily exclaimed the crowd. 'That's him over there, leaning against yonder tree.'

Rip looked and saw a precise copy of himself as he was when he climbed the mountain the day before: evidently just as lazy and certainly as ragged. It must be his son!

Poor Rip was now completely confounded. Was he who he thought he was? Could he be another man? Was he, maybe, dead?

In the midst of these depressing thoughts, a fellow in a cocked hat demanded who he was and what was his name.

'God knows,' said Rip. 'I'm not myself today. I was last night. If that's me over yonder—no, it can't be. I'm standing here in my own shoes. You see, I fell asleep upon the mountain last night and when I woke up someone had changed my gun. They changed me too. I just don't know who I am!'

The bystanders began to look at one another knowingly; some tapped their heads, winked and nodded. Just then a fresh-faced, comely woman pressed through the throng to get a peep at the odd old man. She had a child in her arms who began to cry on seeing the wild-looking, long-bearded figure.

'Hush, Rip,' the woman cried. 'That old man won't hurt you. He's harmless.'

169

The name of the child, the tone of the mother's voice and the way she held herself, seemed to waken a chord of recognition in Rip's mind.

'What's your name?' asked Rip excited.

'Judith Gardenier,' she replied.

'And your father's name?' asked Rip.

'Rip Van Winkle was his name but, poor man, it's twenty years since he left home with his dog and gun and was never seen again. His dog came home without him. Nobody knows whether he shot himself or was carried off by Red Indians. I was only a little girl then.'

Rip had but one question more to ask. He put it in a faltering voice: 'And your mother?'

'Oh, she died a short time since. She broke a blood vessel in a fit of temper at a New England pedlar.'

Well, there was one crumb of comfort then in this strange situation! The old man could now restrain himself no longer. He flung his arms about his daughter and her child and, with tears streaming down his grizzled cheeks, he shouted, 'I am your father! Rip Van Winkle! Young once, now old. Doesn't anybody know poor Rip Van Winkle?'

All stood amazed, until an old woman tottered out from among the crowd and peered into his face.

'Sure enough,' she cried. 'It is himself. It's Rip Van Winkle. Welcome home, neighbour. Where have you been these twenty long years?'

Rip's story was soon told, for the twenty years had been to him but as one night. The crowd stared when they heard it. Some winked at one another, some put their tongues in their cheeks. But there was no doubt that Rip Van Winkle had returned from somewhere after twenty years.

To make a long story short, Rip's daughter took him home to live with her. She had a comfortable house and farm, and her husband was a cheery sort whom Rip remembered as an urchin who used to climb upon his back. As to Rip's idle son, who was the image of himself, he was given work to do on the farm, though he showed no more interest in his own affairs than the elder Rip had done.

Rip now resumed his old walks and habits. He took his place once more on the bench at the inn door, and was looked upon with reverence as a chronicler of the old

days 'before the war'. Of course, he was fond of telling
his tale to every stranger that arrived at Mr Doolittle's
hotel. Every time he told it, the story seemed to vary in
its detail. But the basic plot remained the same, as I have
told it here.

Even to this day, the descendants of Dutch colonists
living in the Catskill Mountains never hear a thunder-
storm without saying that the noise must be Rip's
companions playing skittles in their mountain hall. And
it is the wish of many hen-pecked husbands in the
neighbourhood, when life hangs heavy on their hands,
that they might take a comforting drink from Rip Van
Winkle's flagon.

Anaeet

One spring morning, Prince Vachagan of Armenia went hunting and, in the course of the day, he came to the village of Atsik. Tired and footsore, he sat by a well to rest. While he was resting a group of village girls came to the well, filling their pitchers with the pure spring water.

One of the girls offered a drink to the handsome wayfarer, seeing that he was thirsty. But just as he was about to drink, another girl snatched the pitcher from him and emptied the water into a pail. Then she refilled the pitcher from the pail, only to pour it back into the pail again. This she did six or seven times.

In the meantime Vachagan's throat became parched. He was so eager for a drink, and the girl seemed to be teasing him. However, at last she handed him a little water in a pitcher.

The prince greedily drank the water, then asked, 'Why did you not give me water the first time? Why did you tease me when I was so thirsty?'

'It is not our custom to tease a stranger,' the girl replied. 'You were tired and hot; the cold water would have harmed you. That is why I waited before letting you drink.'

The girl's reply surprised and pleased Vachagan as much as did her beauty. When he asked her name, she replied, 'I am Anaeet, daughter of Aran the shepherd. And you, stranger, who might you be?'

The prince hesitated, at last saying, 'I cannot tell you that. But, I give my promise, you will learn soon enough who I am and where I come from.'

172

So saying, the prince left her at the well. He returned directly to the palace and told his mother that he wished to marry the shepherd's wise and lovely daughter.

His mother, the queen, would not hear of it. 'My dear son,' she said, 'a prince should not wed a mere shepherdess. The Afghan King has three fair daughters, you may choose a bride from among them. The King of Georgia has two lovely daughters, choose one as you wish. The Prince of Gugar has one beautiful daughter; should you marry her you would be heir to all her father's lands. No less beautiful is the daughter of the Prince of Sunik. All these princesses are worthy of you.'

But Vachagan would marry none but the humble Anaeet. So stubborn was he and so sad did he become, that in the end his parents despatched Shivar, their son's faithful servant, to the village of Atsik.

Aran the shepherd welcomed Shivar and spread a carpet before him. Upon this carpet the prince's envoy spread the royal gifts: silk robes and precious jewels.

'Why is the king's son so gracious to me?' asked Anaeet, when Shivar had explained that the gifts were for her.

'Vachagan, only son to our noble king, met you one day at the well and fell in love with you,' said Shivar. 'I am here by order of the king to ask you to wed the prince.'

'Then the hunter I met was indeed the prince?' Anaeet mused. 'He seemed a good man. What trade does he know?'

'He is the king's son!' said Shivar surprised. 'All the king's subjects are his servants. What need does a prince have of a trade?'

'Who is master today may be servant tomorrow,' replied Anaeet softly. 'Everyone should have a trade, be he king, prince or pauper.'

Shivar was surprised at her words and not a little angry. 'Then you will not wed the prince because he has no trade?' he asked.

'That is so,' the girl said. 'Take back all your gifts and tell the prince to pardon me: I would not marry a man who has no trade.'

At the palace, the news was brought to the king and queen, who could scarcely conceal their relief. Surely, now their son would change his mind.

But Vachagan simply said, 'Anaeet is quite right. I too must learn a trade, like all people.'

Reluctantly, the king summoned a council of his nobles to select a suitable calling for his son. After much deliberation, they resolved that the weaving of brocade was the most fitting profession for a prince. A skilled craftsman was forthwith brought from Persia and within a year Vachagan had learned the craft. Using fine gold thread, he wove a length of delicate brocade and sent his faithful Shivar with it to Anaeet.

She received it graciously and immediately gave consent to their marriage. Preparations for the wedding were at once begun, and the grand festivities lasted full seven days. The married pair were very happy.

Soon after the wedding, however, a mystery occurred that clouded their lives for a time. Shivar, the prince's faithful friend and servant, disappeared without trace. Though people searched high and low for him, not a sign of his whereabouts could be discovered. As the years rolled on, memory of him dimmed and other events claimed attention: the king and queen both died in their declining years, and Vachagan became king. Never had the people been ruled so justly as by King Vachagan and his wise Queen Anaeet.

One day, however, the lovely Anaeet said to her husband, 'I perceive, my dear Vachagan, that you know your subjects poorly. Your nobles do not tell you the entire truth; they would have you believe that all goes well at all times. Perchance that is not so? Would it not be wise to go about your kingdom now and then, in the guise of a merchant or a craftsman and talk freely with your subjects?'

'You are right, wise Anaeet,' said the king. 'I knew my people better when I was a prince and hunted across the countryside. But who would rule while I'm away?'

'I would,' his wife replied. 'No one need know that you are gone.'

So it was decided between them. King Vachagan dressed as a simple peasant and started out on his travels. There was much he learned to his advantage in seeing how the poor folk lived and in listening to the village gossip. Finally, one day he arrived at the town of Perozh.

As he sat resting in the market square, he noticed a crowd of people following a venerable priest. The old priest moved slowly: his way was first cleared with a brush and stepping stones were placed beneath his feet. So pious was the priest that he would not even step on the ground for fear of crushing an ant or beetle.

A rug was spread in the square for the priest to rest, and Vachagan pushed through the throng to gain a better view of him. Though aged, the priest still had sharp eyes and saw at once that a stranger was in their midst.

'Who are you?' he asked Vachagan. 'And what is your trade?'

'I am a weaver just arrived from distant parts,' the king explained to the old priest.

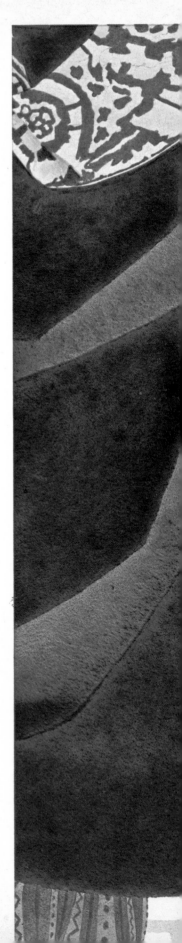

'Good, then you shall come with me,' said the other.
'I'll pay you well and treat you kindly.'

While they were conversing, other holy men had gone
off in different directions and shortly returned with
bearers laden down with supplies of every sort. When all
the holy men were assembled, the chief priest rose and
left the square. Obediently and with some curiosity,
Vachagan followed them.

When the procession came to the city gates, the priest
turned to bless the crowd before it dispersed. Then the
holy men, the bearers and Vachagan continued on their
way beyond the town. After some time they arrived at a
high stone wall in which there was a single door. The

venerable priest unlocked it and the procession passed through.

A large square lay within; in the centre stood a great temple built of red stone. The bearers set down their bundles as instructed before being led, along with Vachagan, behind the temple to an iron door that led into a hillside cavern.

'Go in, friends,' said the priest. 'You will find work within and you will be rewarded as you deserve.'

They entered silently, each and every one. Behind them they heard the iron door swing to with a great clang, shutting out the light. Their only way now was forward; so they stumbled on down a tunnel until they

reached a large cave. In the cave the air was rent continually by the most pitiful human groans and screams.

The newcomers stared about them in growing horror, as their gaze alighted upon what looked like human skeletons rotting away along the walls.

A figure staggered towards them resembling neither man nor beast. It had all the features of a corpse, with sunken eyes, a death's head and skeletal frame. It was a human being all right, but in a sorry state.

'Come with me,' a hollow voice spoke from the emaciated frame, 'and I shall show you everything.'

The dozen men followed him down a narrow tunnel and came into a second cave filled with men writhing in their death throes. In a third cave stood enormous pots on great fires. Vachagan, bolder than his companions, bent over one pot and instantly turned away in horror, saying nothing to the others. They were then led along another stone tunnel where, in the dim half-light, they saw several hundred men toiling without cease, all of them as pitiful as the guide. Some were weaving, some sewing, some embroidering, some knitting.

Said the corpse-like guide, 'That evil priest who led you here lured us to our doom in the same way. I do not know how many years I have spent here, for there is neither day nor night, just this eternal gloom. All I know is that my companions are long dead. If a man has a trade he is taken and given work until he dies; if he has none, he is thrown into an iron pot and boiled alive, as you have seen.'

As the gaunt figure was speaking, his voice and features struck a faint chord in Vachagan's memory. Yes, it was none other than his old friend and servant Shivar. But Vachagan made no sign of recognition for fear of snapping the slender thread that bound his long-lost friend to life.

When Shivar had moved away, Vachagan asked his companions what work they could do. One was a tailor, one a weaver, the rest had no trade at all.

Just then steps were heard coming down the tunnel, and a priest appeared accompanied by armed guards.

'You, newcomers, which of you knows a trade?' asked the priest roughly.

'We all do,' Vachagan replied. 'We work together,

weaving precious brocade which is a hundred times more valuable than gold.'

The priest looked unconvinced, yet nonetheless ordered tools and materials to be brought for the men to prove themselves.

'But should your boast be less than true,' he warned, 'I shall have you all skinned alive and boiled in oil!'

Vachagan set to work, instructing his helpers in their craft. In the passing of time they had woven a most splendid brocade embroidered with a message that told of all the horrors of the underground dungeon. But the message was hidden in the pattern and could only be read and understood by those wise enough to interpret it.

The priest was delighted with Vachagan's craftsmanship.

'I told you that our brocade was a hundred times more precious than gold,' Vachagan told the priest. 'In truth, it is worth much more than that amount, for certain charms are woven into the pattern that cannot be understood by ordinary folk. Only the all-wise Queen Anaeet will appreciate their meaning.'

The greedy priest was amazed and made up his mind to sell the brocade himself, so that none should share in his profit. Without a word to the high priest, he took the brocade and set out alone for the palace of Queen Anaeet.

Meanwhile, Queen Anaeet had ruled the country wisely, and no one suspected that the king was away. Nevertheless, as the days passed into weeks and even months, and still there was no sign of her husband's return, Anaeet became alarmed.

One morning she was informed of the arrival of a priest bearing precious wares. Once admitted to the queen's presence, he laid before her the length of magnificent brocade. Anaeet gave it the briefest glance without noticing the pattern.

'What price are you asking?' she asked.

'It is three hundred times more valuable than gold, O Queen,' he answered. 'It has special charms embroidered in the pattern.'

Anaeet unfolded the brocade to take a closer look. On it she saw no charms, but letters woven into the pattern so artfully that they formed whole words. Anaeet read the message in excitement:

"My own dear Anaeet, I am held captive in an underground cavern. The bearer of this brocade is my cruel guard. Shivar is with me. Send an army to rescue us; we are just east of Perozh in a hillside cavern that lies behind a temple enclosed by high walls. Without your help we shall all perish soon, Vachagan."

Anaeet at once gave an order for the surprised priest to be seized and locked up. Then her heralds rang out the alarm, summoning all the townsfolk to the palace.

'Hear me, citizens,' shouted Anaeet. 'The life of your king is in peril. Let all who love him follow me to rescue him. By midday we must reach the town of Perozh.'

Within the hour, all the men and women of the town were armed and mounted on their horses, eager to follow Anaeet to rescue their king. They did not stop their gallop until they reached the market square in Perozh a little before midday. Once there, Anaeet ordered the town governor to lead her army forthwith to the temple beyond the city walls.

Thinking that more prisoners had been brought, the priests unlocked the iron gate to let in Anaeet and her army. Only then did they realise their mistake.

The chief priest rushed forward sword in hand and

would surely have struck down the bold Anaeet had her horse not reared up and trampled him to death. The doors of the underground cavern were then flung open.

A fearful sight met the people's gaze. Ghost-like apparitions crawled out of the hole. Some, at death's door, hobbled along on crutches, blinded by the daylight. The more recent arrivals staggered about drunkenly like crippled ants. The last to emerge were Vachagan and Shivar, the king supporting his friend lest he fall.

How happy Anaeet and Vachagan were to see each other again. And how grateful was the faithful Shivar. He wept and pressed his lips to Queen Anaeet's hand.

'Our dear Queen Anaeet,' he cried. 'Today you have saved our lives.'

'Not so, my brother,' Vachagan told him. 'Anaeet saved us long ago the day she asked you if the king's son had a trade. Do you remember how you scorned her question? We owe our lives to her wisdom.'

Throughout the wide lands of Armenia the tidings spread of King Vachagan's terrible adventure. And all gave praise to the king and his resourceful queen. The minstrels made up songs about them, and thus the story of Anaeet's wisdom has come to us today.

The Little Match Girl

Once, in a town in Denmark, on the very last evening of the year, New Year's Eve, the snow began to fall and it became bitterly cold.

Through the cold and gloom walked a little girl; both her head and her feet were bare, for she was very poor. It is true that she'd had a pair of shoes when she left home that morning, but they were her mother's and so were much too big for her. They had slipped off as she ran across the road to dodge two speeding carriages. One shoe was not to be found anywhere and the other was snatched up by a boy who ran off with it, saying he'd use it as a cradle.

So now the little girl walked barefoot through the snow. Her feet were sore and raw red with cold. In her hands she was carrying a small bundle of matches and there were a good many more matches in her tattered apron pocket. Nobody had bought any all day long, or given her so much as a penny. Cold and hungry, she walked on through the city.

Snowflakes fell on the long fair tresses that curled in pretty ringlets on her shoulders, but she didn't notice them. As she walked, she looked in the lighted windows of the houses she passed. The smell of roast goose came

to her from several homes. Many families were celebrating New Year's Eve together.

In a narrow alley between two great houses she sat down, tucking her tiny bare feet beneath her. It did no good; she could bring no warmth back to her toes. She did not dare go home, for she had sold no matches, earned no money, and she was afraid her father would beat her. Besides, her home was not much warmer than the street. She lived in an attic beneath a broken roof, and the wind whistled through it, even though they had tried to block the biggest holes with bits of straw and tattered rags.

Her little hands were numb from cold. Perhaps, she thought, if she lit a match it might warm them. If she but dared! Well, she did. She drew one out and struck it against the wall of the house. Oh, how warm it was and how brightly burned the match, just like a tiny candle. She cupped it in her hands. How funny! She fancied she was sitting before a big iron stove with a fire blazing inside it. How beautifully warm it was! She poked out her toes so that they too could have some warmth. But, alas, in that instant, the flame died, the stove vanished and she sat alone with a burnt match in her hand.

She lit another. Its flame lit up the wall and somehow made it transparent like a veil, so that she could see right through, into the house. She saw a table spread with a snow-white cloth and set with the very finest china dishes. In one dish was a roast goose stuffed with apples and delicious plums. Then—lo and behold!—that goose, knife and fork and all, jumped down from the table and came waddling towards her. The little girl stretched out her arms, but the match went out, and her hands touched instead the cold, hard wall beside her.

She struck a third match. It flared up, and by its light she saw that she was sitting under a lovely Christmas tree; it was even grander than the ones she'd seen on Christmas Eve through the windows of the wealthy merchants' houses. Hundreds of candles burned on its green branches, and bright little figures like those she'd seen in toyshop windows looked down upon her. She smiled and reached towards them in delight. But at that moment the match went out and she saw that the candles on the Christmas tree were only bright stars in the sky. One star fell, its trail blazing a line of fire across the sombre heavens.

'Someone is dying,' murmured the little girl sadly. For

her grannie had told her that a shooting star was a human soul on its way to heaven.

She struck another match against the wall and in its light she saw her grannie, the only person in her life who'd been kind and loving to her. Her grannie had been dead these two years past. Yet now she was there, stretching out her arms to the little match girl.

'Grannie,' the little girl cried out, 'please take me with you. I know you'll leave me when the match goes out, just like the nice warm stove, the waddling goose, and the lovely Christmas tree!'

Hastily, she lit all the remaining matches in her bundle, lest her grannie disappear. The matches burned with such a bright, strong flame that night became as light as day. Never, the child thought, had her grannie looked so happy. Then her grandmother took the little girl in her arms and flew up with her to where there is no more cold, no more hunger, no more pain.

In the cold glimmer of morning someone found the little match girl curled up in the narrow alleyway. She had frozen to death on the last night of the old year. The sun of a new year now shone down upon her lifeless body; her lap was filled with burnt-out matches.

Basil Fet Frumos

A fact is a fact, a tale a tale.
Where no one passed, there runs no trail.
A plant not planted bears no seeds.
What did not happen, no rumour breeds.

Once upon a time in Romania there lived a man with his
wife, and they had a daughter as lovely as the sky at
dawn. She was quick and nimble with her hands, and as
spirited as a fresh spring breeze.

One fine day, this lovely daughter took two pitchers
down to the well to fetch some water. Her pitchers filled,
she rested awhile and noticed a sprig of pale green
basil growing inside the well. Without a thought, she
plucked the plant and put it to her nose to inhale the
delicate perfume. And from its fresh, magic fragrance
she conceived a child.

When her parents found out that their daughter was
with child, they were very angry and drove her out. She,
poor girl, made her way without a halt into a dense forest
until at last she came upon a cave. Weary from her
walking, she sat down to rest just inside the entrance, out
of the cold wind. All of a sudden, she gave a start; she
heard a coughing and wheezing from the depths of the
forest cave and, coming towards her on spindly legs, she
saw an old, old man with a beard so long it touched his
knees, and hair that reached down to his heels.

'Who are you, girl?' the old man asked, peering at her
from under eyebrows so bushy he had to lift them with a
crook to see her.

Too terrified to answer, the girl burst into tears, hiding
her face in her hands.

The old hermit sat her down on a stone bench and
calmed her with kind words. Like rain that cools the soil
after the sun's burning heat, so old people's words may
sometimes be a balm to the troubled spirits of the young.
Comforted, the girl soon told her story and gladly
accepted the old hermit's kind invitation to stay in the
cave for as long as she wished.

Thus they lived, the girl finding solace in her grief, the old man company in his declining years.

Time passed swiftly. The girl gave birth to a child so fair that even the sun smiled on him as it gazed down from the heavens. The old hermit was overjoyed, his heart grew as light as it was when he was young.

The moment the child was born, the old man bathed him in the morning dew so that no evil would befall him. As a birthday gift, he gave the child a stout club and sharp sword left over from the valiant days of his own youth. The proud mother gave her son the name of Basil, after the plant that she had plucked from the well and to this name the hermit added Fet Frumos, Brave and Strong, that the boy might grow up to know no fear.

Time flew by, the old hermit died, and Basil Fet Frumos grew to manhood. He became a fine hunter, bringing his mother plentiful meat to eat and wild berries whose sweet juices she might drink. Besides, he cheered her life with happy songs and exciting stories of his adventures in the forest.

One day, when Basil was out hunting in distant cedar groves and forests of larch, he came to a narrow pass leading down into a wooded valley. As he gazed into the distance he saw what seemed to be a great silver lake in which the sun was bathing. Coming closer, he saw it was not a lake at all, but a palace of pure gold studded with giant pearls that sparkled and glittered amidst the verdant forest. Never in his life had he beheld such beauty.

Entering the palace he passed through many chambers, yet nowhere did he see a sign of life. As he wandered through the palace gardens he suddenly heard a crashing and roaring from the forest behind the palace. Then, out of the trees, came seven fearsome-looking dragons, eyes full of venom and mouths full of fire. Across each of their backs lay three men, bound tightly hand and foot.

As Basil hid behind the palace door, the seven dragons entered with their prey, lit a great fire beneath a giant cauldron and, when the water was boiling, they threw their captives into the pot, adding salt and spices to their taste. Then, when the men were cooked, the dragons ate them, bones and all, licking their greedy lips and crunching every last morsel. Just as they completed their

repast, one dragon chanced to look round and caught sight of Basil behind the door.

'There's another human ready for our pot!' it roared. Thereupon, all seven dragons leapt up and rushed at Basil Fet Frumos. But he was unafraid. He swung his stout club so fast it was a blur before the dazed dragons' eyes, and he swung his sharp sword so fiercely that, as each dragon came in reach, he cut off its head. In no time at all he had slain six dragons, sending their heads spinning across the floor like fallen apples.

However, Basil's sword could not pierce the thick scaly skin of the seventh dragon at all. It was only when he attacked it with his club that the dragon gave way and fled, trailing its long tail between its legs. It ran down a stone staircase until it reached the dungeons. There, begging for mercy, it plunged into a damp dungeon and slammed shut the iron door. Basil locked the dungeon securely and left the dragon prisoner.

Basil Fet Frumos returned home and told his mother of his adventures. Together, they left the cave forever and went to make their home in the golden palace; at last they could live in comfort and plenty.

Yet just as the gentle warmth of spring can be suddenly destroyed by violent storms, so was the peace and happiness of Basil Fet Frumos and his mother shattered. Those seven dragons had served the evil Cloantsa, an old witch with a heart as black as pitch and a face so mean she could wither a flower merely by staring at it. When her dragons failed to return, she writhed and twisted like a snake cast into fire, and she decided to make her way to the palace to discover what had happened.

At the time Cloantsa arrived, Basil was out hunting in the forest while his mother prepared a dinner. The poor mother was no match for the evil Cloantsa, and was quickly locked up in the dungeon in the dragon's place. Learning the story from her seventh dragon, the evil

witch knew she would have to summon up all her wiles and cunning to defeat Basil Fet Frumos. So she concealed the dragon, and then spun herself like a top, taking the form of Basil's mother.

When Basil returned he noticed nothing amiss.

'My dearest son,' the witch said, 'I feel most unwell and will surely die unless you can bring me a cup of bird's milk.'

Basil was ready to do anything to save his mother, so he set off in search of bird's milk, though, truth to tell, he knew not where to look.

On and on he walked, through forest and over plain, until at last he came to a tall cottage on a hillside surrounded by a high fence. As he knocked at the gate, he was surprised to hear a clear young voice call to him.

'If, young man, you come with pure heart, then enter freely. If not, beware, my hounds will tear you to pieces.'

'I have no ill intent, dear lady,' answered Basil.

The gate swung open of its own accord and Basil passed through into a garden set before a beautifully-carved wooden house. Entering the house, Basil saw a maiden sitting in a chair before the table.

'Good morrow, gracious lady,' he said.

'Good morrow to you, bold youth,' the maiden replied.

How beautiful she was. The stars, the moon, and the silver rays of dawn would all look pale before her beauty. Basil's heart beat faster, for he had never in his life beheld such a beautiful maiden.

With a graceful wave, she beckoned him to the table, and as they supped he told her of his quest for bird's milk and the strange sickness of his mother.

'Sadly, I know of no such milk,' the maiden said. 'But I perceive that you are good, so I shall ask my brother, who knows of all such mysteries, where it may be found.'

That was how Basil Fet Frumos came to meet Ilana Cosintsana, sister to the Sun.

When her guest was fast asleep, Ilana went to her brother and asked him where the milk could be found.

'Far away, little sister, far away,' the Sun replied. 'The way is to the east beyond the Copper Mountain. There upon a crag lives a monster bird with wings like thunder clouds. She has the bird's milk and feeds it to her young.

192

But
be warned:
she is a ferocious
creature who feeds
off human flesh.'
Ilana Cosintsana, sister
to the Sun, felt pity for the bold
young man who would be going to a certain doom, so she
helped him as best she could. Leading out a twelve-
winged steed from her stables, she presented it to Basil
and sent him on his way.

Before departing, Basil thanked the lovely maiden
warmly, then leapt upon the twelve-winged steed and
rode off like the wind. It was not long before he sighted
Copper Mountain and, beyond it, the lofty crag on which
that monster bird had its home. Arriving at the foot of
the lofty crag, Basil looked up and up, for the crag's peak
disappeared into the sky. But there right near the top
Basil spotted the monster bird, its enormous wings
almost shutting out the daylight.

Basil's mount leapt from one rock to another, climbing
up the sheer wall of the lofty crag and when it had almost
reached the peak, it stopped, allowing Basil to dismount.
The sight that met him made his eyes sore with looking.
For in a nest like a gigantic copper bowl sat the monster
bird's young, the size of great oxen, opening their
massive beaks for the milk their mother would shortly
bring.

Hiding in a narrow crevice with his steed, Basil held
his breath and lay in wait. He did not have long to bide
his time, for soon the mother bird came flying down to
feed milk to her gluttonous offspring. As she dived down
to the nest, Basil darted forward and held his pitcher
beneath the bird. Quite unaware, that monster bird let
her milk pour freely into the pitcher. As soon as the jug
was full, Basil quickly jumped on his horse and rode
down the mountainside with the monster bird in hot
pursuit. But having only one pair of wings, she could not
catch the twelve-winged horse which flew fast and true
back to the home of Ilana Cosintsana.

On his return, Basil ate and drank and bathed, then
went to bed. While he was sleeping soundly, the sister to

the Sun, who knew much more than her bold guest, replaced the bird's milk with the creamy milk of a common goat.

Next morning, Basil Fet Frumos took up his pitcher and, thanking the kind maiden once again, he bade her farewell and rode back on the twelve-winged steed to his sick mother.

As soon as she saw him coming, the witch Cloantsa writhed and twisted like a serpent pierced by fiery arrows. But she made out she was glad to see him and eagerly drank the common goat's milk.

'Dearest son,' she said, 'you have made me well again. Now you must rest from your tiring journey. Come, lie down and sleep.'

Unsuspecting, Basil lay down upon a couch and went to sleep. No sooner had his eyes closed than the evil witch jumped out of bed and began spinning like a top. Soon she had taken her ugly, evil form again. Then, summoning her dragon from its hiding place, she commanded it to tear the youth to pieces.

Snorting joyfully, the dragon rushed forward to take its revenge. It quickly overpowered the exhausted Basil and shredded his body like a head of cabbage. Then, gathering up the many pieces, it packed them into two saddle bags upon the twelve-winged steed's back and slapped its haunches.

'Away, old nag,' it roared. 'Whence you bore him living, thence you bear him dead!'

At once the steed flew off like the wind, back to the

home of Ilana Cosintsana. Finding to her horror the
remains of Basil Fet Frumos, she went in haste to her
larder and snatched up the pitcher full of bird's milk.
Carefully, she washed each broken bone and torn piece
of flesh in the bird's milk, then fitted each and every
piece together until the young man was whole again.
Once more she bathed him in the milk and gave him
what remained to drink. With each sip he gained new
strength and soon was stronger than ever he was before.

Like hailstones falling from the sky, such was the
vengeance beating in Basil's breast. With Ilana Cosintsana, he flew to the golden palace upon the twelve-
winged horse. When they arrived, the evil witch and her
dragon were feasting merrily at the banquet table, served
by Basil's grieving mother. The moment they set eyes on
Basil entering the hall, their eyes popped out in fear.
Before they had time to move, Basil had taken up his
sharp sword and struck them dead, chopped up their
bodies, burned each evil piece and scattered their ashes
far and wide across the land.

That task accomplished, he embraced his dear mother
and the lovely Ilana. And in the way of all good stories,
the two young people were presently wed and held a
wedding feast the like of which was never seen. At the
head of the table in the golden palace sat the Sun himself,
drinking whole kegs of wine and merrily wishing long life
and good cheer to the radiant pair.

So they all lived in love and happiness and they live on
still—so long, that is, that the time has not arrived for
them to die.

Dafydd and the Lady of the Lake

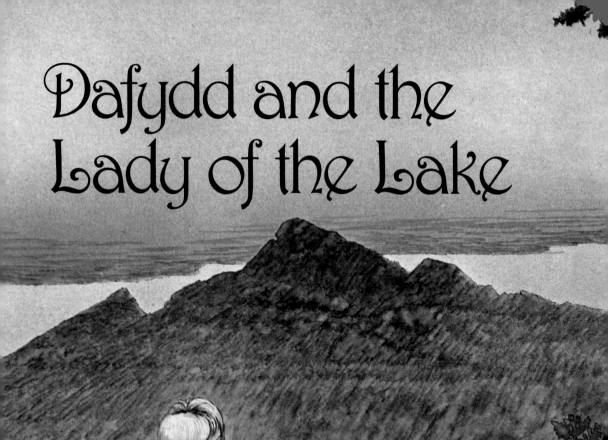

High in a hollow in the Black Mountains of South Wales is a lonely sheet of water known as Llyn y Fan Fach.

In a farm across the hills from this lake there once lived a widow with her only son whose name was Dafydd. When the boy was old enough to look after the cows, he would often take them to graze in the sweet grass by the lake.

One day, as Dafydd was sitting by the water, watching the cows cropping the lush grass, he was surprised to hear a soft splashing noise coming from the lake. He looked around and, to his astonishment, saw a young maiden standing in the calm smooth water, her skin the colour of creamy dew, her hair burnished by the sun's golden rays.

She was the most beautiful person he had ever set eyes on as she stood there in the lake, combing her long tresses with a golden comb and using the smooth surface of the lake as her mirror.

Dafydd ran to the very edge of the lake, unable to believe his eyes. As he gazed longingly at her, he held out the crust and cheese that was his lunch. He had nothing else to offer. The lady of the lake looked up from her combing and came slowly gliding over the lake towards him. But she shook her head at his offering, saying:

> 'Cras dy fara,
> Nid hawdd fy nala.
> You with the crust of bread,
> Cannot have me to wed.'

With that she dived under the water.

With heavy heart, Dafydd made his way home. He told his mother of the lovely vision he had seen, and as they pondered together over the strange words uttered by the lady of the lake, they finally decided that they must be a spell to do with the crust of bread.

'Next time you go to the lake,' the mother advised her son, 'you should take some "toes" with you.'

Next morning, long before the sun's rays shone above the crest of the mountain, Dafydd was standing by the lake with the "toes", or unbaked bread, in his hand, anxiously waiting for the maiden to appear. The sun slowly rose in the heavens, scattering the mists shrouding the mountain tops.

Hour after hour, the lad stared into the waters, and hour after hour there was nothing to be seen save the ripples raised by the breeze and the sunbeams dancing upon them. By late afternoon, he was ready to turn his footsteps homewards when, to his great joy, the maiden again appeared above the sunlit waters of the lake.

She was even more lovely than before, and Dafydd, forgetting in his admiration of her beauty all the words that he had carefully prepared, held out the unbaked dough.

But with a shake of her lovely head, the lake maiden refused the gift as before, adding:

'Llaith dy fara,
Ti ni fynna.
You with the unbaked bread,
Cannot have me to wed.'

This time, before vanishing under the water, she smiled such a gracious smile that Dafydd's heart overflowed with love. As he walked home, the remembrance of her smile consoled him with the hope that when next she appeared she might not refuse his gift.

He told his mother all that had happened, and together they wondered on the meaning of it all. Since the lady had refused both crust and unbaked dough, they decided that, perhaps, she would accept half-baked bread should it be offered.

So next day, long before first light, Dafydd was walking the water margin of the lake with half-baked bread in his hand, staring fixedly into the smooth waters.

The red sun rose, but it was not strong enough to disperse the mist hanging over the mountains, and rain began to fall. But still the young lad heeded nothing as he stared at the water. Morning wore on to afternoon, and afternoon to evening. But nothing was to be seen save the scudding waves and the rain dimples in the dark waters.

Shades of night began to fall, and Dafydd was about to depart in bitter disappointment when, casting a last glance across the lake, he suddenly saw some jet black cows walking on the water. The sight of these dark beasts raised his hopes. Perhaps, he thought, they would be followed by the lake maiden herself. And sure enough, it was not long before she emerged from the water.

Dafydd was almost beside himself with joy at her appearance. His happiness increased when he saw that she was walking towards him on the water. As she came nearer, he waded into the cool waters of the lake to meet her, holding out the half-baked bread.

This time she took his gift with a grateful smile, and even allowed him to lead her by the hand on to the shore. When she was standing there beside him, her beauty seemed even more dazzling than before, and Dafydd completely lost his tongue. With bowed head and scarlet cheeks, he just stared shyly at her feet, noticing, without thinking about it, that her left sandal lace was broken.

At long last he recovered his wits and, looking straight into her hazel eyes, said, 'Dear lady of the lake, I love you more than I can tell and would beg you to be my wife.'

At first she was taken aback by this bold declaration. But he pleaded with her so earnestly that in the end she gave her promise to be his bride. There was, however, one condition.

'I shall marry you,' she said, 'and I shall live with you, until you strike me three clear blows without a cause.'

Of course, Dafydd protested that he could never strike her. He said that he would sooner cut off his hand than employ it in such a way.

As he was making his protestations, she suddenly ran from him and, in an instant, had dived into the lake. Thinking that she had teased him cruelly and was now gone forever, Dafydd was so grief-stricken that he resolved to live no longer.

He hastened to the top of a large rock overhanging the lake and was about to jump into the water's depths when he heard a shout—'Stay, bold youth, come here.'

As he turned, he saw a white-haired old man, as regal as a king, accompanied by two lovely maidens. Dafydd descended from the overhanging rock and came before them.

'You wish to wed one of my daughters,' the old man said. 'So be it. I shall not oppose you, for my daughter says she's willing. But first, to prove your love, you must tell me the one you've pledged to marry.'

Dafydd's heart felt light. How could he fail to recognise his beloved lady of the lake! Yet when he looked at the two maidens, he was confused: they were as perfectly alike as two droplets of water. The two young maids were of exactly the same size, with slanting hazel eyes, long copper-coloured tresses, and were both clad in long white shifts. They were such perfect copies that it was quite impossible to tell them apart.

The thought that he might pronounce wrongly all but drove Dafydd to distraction and stayed his pointing finger. He had almost given up the task in despair when one of the two maidens moved her left foot slightly forward. This motion, as slight as it was, did not escape his eager eyes, and looking down he noticed the torn sandal lace upon the dainty foot. With a cry of triumph, he immediately took her hand.

'You have chosen rightly,' said the stern old man. 'Be a kind and loving husband to her and I shall grant as dowry as many cows, sheep, goats, pigs and horses as she can count in a single breath. But mind you this—should you but strike three needless blows, then she shall return to me forever.'

Dafydd was overjoyed. Once again he protested that he would sooner cut off his hand than offend his beloved bride. With a knowing smile upon his lips, the old man turned to his daughter and bade her count the number of cows she wished to have. And she began to count in fives—one, two, three, four, five—one, two, three, four, five—one, two, three, four, five—as many times as she could until her breath gave out. Straightaway, as many cows as she had counted came lowing from the lake. Then she counted the sheep—one, two, three, four, five—one, two, three, four, five—one, two, three, four, five—she went on counting until she had to draw a breath. In the twinkling of an eye, as many sheep as she had counted came bleating from the lake. In the same way, she counted goats, pigs and horses and an equal team of every kind ranged themselves upon the shore.

The old man and his second daughter meanwhile had vanished, and Dafydd took his lady's hand and led her to his farm. All the animals followed behind.

In the passing of the days Dafydd and his bride were married amid much rejoicing. Time went by in perfect bliss, and three handsome sons were born to them.

When the youngest boy was ten years old, Dafydd and his wife Nelferch—for that was the lake maiden's name—were invited to a wedding in the next village,

They started out for the wedding walking from their farm. The day was hot, the distance far, and soon Nelferch was footsore, complaining she could walk no farther.

'If you do not wish to walk all the way,' Dafydd said, 'then I shall return home and fetch a horse for you.'

His wife consented, and asked him to bring her gloves which she had left behind. He returned home, brought the horse and gloves, and was more than a little tired and hot from his exertions.

As he went to help his wife sit astride the horse, she suddenly said, 'I've changed my mind. Let us go back home at once.'

At this unexpected turn, Dafydd lost his temper and, before he could stop himself, had struck her with the gloves, saying, 'Dos, dos, Nelferch! Go on, go on, Nelferch!'

His wife mounted the horse and sighed deeply. 'That, my husband, is the first needless blow,' she said, and she reminded him of the promise he had given when he pledged to wed her.

Though he was bitterly angry with himself, Dafydd consoled himself with the fact that he still had two chances left and he promised himself that he would never strike his wife again.

Several years later, they were both invited to a local christening. It was such a merry, jovial occasion that Dafydd was much astonished when his wife suddenly burst into tears and sobbed as if her heart would break. All the assembled company stared at her.

'What is wrong with you, dear wife?' asked Dafydd gently.

'I weep,' she said, 'because this poor child will suffer great agony during its stay on earth. And it will shortly die.'

The guests were all amazed and some were angry at such unguarded words uttered before the newborn babe and its parents. Dafydd, who had drunk more than one glass of wholesome home brew, flushed red and shook his wife firmly by the shoulder.

Nelferch stopped weeping and gazed sadly at her husband through tear-filled eyes.

'O my husband,' she sighed, 'you have struck the second needless blow.'

Thenceforth, Dafydd was on his guard day and night. He was so happy in his love for Nelferch that he knew his heart would break if another chance blow took her from him.

Some time later, the child whose christening they had attended died after an illness of great pain and suffering. It happened exactly as Nelferch had foretold. Dafydd and his wife went to the funeral and in the very middle of the service, Nelferch began to laugh so loudly that all the mourners stared at her in disbelief.

Her shocked husband was appalled at this lack of consideration for the grieving parents and he whispered loudly to her, 'Hush, wife, have a thought for the poor parents!'

But his wife laughed more loudly than before. In his confusion and embarrassment, Dafydd, without thinking, smacked her face to cure her of these hysterics.

At once he realised what he'd done and hid his face in his hands.

Nelferch stopped laughing at once. Turning to her husband, she said, 'I was laughing with joy because this poor suffering creature has at last been delivered from its great pain and torment. Now, my beloved husband, the last blow has been struck. You had fair warning. I must leave you forever.'

She walked off quickly to the farm and when she arrived, she summoned all the cattle to her, calling each one by name:

'Mu wlfrech, moelfrech,
Mu olfrech, gwynfrech,
Pedair cae tonn-frech,
Yr hen wyneb wen,
A'r las Geigen,
Gyda'r tarw gwyn
O lys y Brenin,
A'r llo du bach,
Sydd ar y bach,
Dere dithe, yn iach adre!

Come, brindled cow, grey freckled,
Come, spotted cow, white speckled,
From your four green meadows suckled,
Ho, old white-face, home again,
Hey, my big grey Geigen,
You, my handsome white bull
Who once in Father's court did rule,
You, my little black calf,
Slain, hung and cut in half,
Become whole and come, you too,
    home again.'

Immediately, they all obeyed the summons of their mistress. Even the little black calf, suspended from the pantry wall, came to life again and, descending from the hook, put on his hide and walked away with the rest of the cows, sheep, goats, pigs and horses. Away they all went, following their mistress to the lake from which they had come those years before.

When they reached the water's edge, they walked in without a halt, each and every one. They disappeared beneath the placid waters. The only trace that was left was a furrow on the bank made by a horse, still drawing a plough with him as he plunged into the lake. This furrow remains there by the lakeside to this day.

All reason now went from Dafydd's life. He followed his wife despairingly down to the lake and, overwhelmed by grief, walked into the lake after her. His body was never found.

The three orphaned sons spent many, many days and nights, keeping a vigil at the lakeside, hoping they might see their lost father and mother once again. Their deep devotion was at last rewarded, for one day, some weeks later, Nelferch appeared alone, gliding over the smooth surface of the lake towards them, just as she had appeared many years before to their father.

She told them to put aside all their grief. She said that henceforth they should have a mission on earth—to relieve the pain and suffering of mankind. Then she took them to a place that, to this day, bears the name of Pant y Meddygon—Doctor's Dell—where healing plants and herbs grow in abundance.

Profiting from their mother's teaching, they became the most skilful healers in the land. They set up in practice at Myddfai for the healing of all those who needed their help, and they willingly gave help free to those who were too poor to pay for aid. From that time, the fame of the healers of Myddfai spread right across the fair green lands of Wales, and is remembered to this day.

The Sweet-Voiced Crocodile

Once upon a time, when the Ancient One lived in the shadow of the green hills, when the sun spirit Arawidi fished in the rivers flowing through the quiet valleys and the branches of the giant coomacka tree touched the sky, there lived on the island of Jamaica a man and his wife with their only daughter. And that girl was so pretty that every young man for miles around came to court her.

But she refused to have any of them. Since she was the only child in the family, she had decided that she would look after her father and mother until they fell into their final sleep. All the same, the lads kept calling at her home, hoping she would change her mind.

At last her father grew impatient with all these love-sick young men calling at his house and decided to hide his daughter for a time, where no one would find her.

'Leah, my daughter,' he said, 'I shall build you a house in the valley where no one will find you. Your mother will bring food each day: breakfast at ten o'clock every morning, dinner at four o'clock every afternoon.'

Thus it was arranged, and when the wooden shack was ready, her parents took the girl under cover of the dark night sky to her new home.

Before she was left alone, her mother told her, 'Listen carefully to me, Leah. Open your door only when you hear me sing this song:

> Leah, Leah, ting-a-ling-ling,
> Honey at the door, darling,
> Sugar at the door, darling,
> Leah, Leah, ting-a-ling-ling.

'When you hear this song you will know I am bringing your meal. On no account open the door to anyone else.'

Now it so happened that Crocodile had observed the building of the house right by his home. And he got mighty curious. Just at that moment he was hiding underneath the wooden shack, listening to all that was said above his head.

As soon as the mother and father had gone, Crocodile crept from his hiding place and crawled to bushes some way from the new house. Then he opened his great jaws and sang as sweetly as he was able:

> 'Leah, Leah, ting-a-ling-ling,
> Honey at the door, darling,
> Sugar at the door, darling,
> Leah, Leah, ting-a-ling-ling.'

The girl was surprised to hear such a fearful rumbling coming from outside.

She called through the window, 'That's not my mother. She doesn't have such a raucous voice. Anyway, it is not time for my meal. I won't open the door.'

Crocodile crawled away crossly. He went straight to the village blacksmith to ask him a favour.

'Brother Blacksmith,' began Crocodile in his rough, low tones. 'I am tired of my raucous voice. I wish to sing sweetly in a high tone.'

The brawny blacksmith took his red hot iron from the forge and held it over Crocodile's mouth.

'The operation is mighty painful,' he said, 'but if you can bear it, Brother Crocodile, open wide and I'll do my best.'

Crocodile opened his great jaws and the blacksmith thrust his red-hot, smoking iron down the gaping throat. The iron hissed and sizzled, and a cloud of steam billowed up and filled the forge. Crocodile leapt halfway to the ceiling with the pain.

When he had recovered, the blacksmith said to him, 'Now, let's hear you sing, Brother Crocodile.'

Crocodile sang in such a high voice that even his own mother would not have recognised him.

'But mark my words well,' the blacksmith said. 'Do not eat any bananas or mangoes. For if you do, your voice will become as rough and raucous as before.'

Crocodile thanked the blacksmith warmly and hurried off, meaning to try out his new voice as soon as possible and eat the pretty Leah. But being a greedy creature, he was by now extremely hungry and his belly rumbled loudly as he waddled quickly through the grass.

Seeing some bananas and juicy mangoes, he said to himself, 'Surely I can eat just one or two. That blacksmith is strong in arm and weak in head. How can I get a rough voice from eating fruit?'

So he ate some fruit, then tried his voice; how horrified he was to hear himself as low and raucous as before the operation.

'Never mind,' he told himself. 'Perhaps the roughness will wear off by the time I reach the shack.'

Just before dinner time, Crocodile arrived at the back of the wooden shack where Leah was living and he opened his great jaws and began to sing:

> 'Leah, Leah, ting-a-ling-ling,
> Honey at the door, darling,
> Sugar at the door, darling,
> Leah, Leah, ting-a-ling-ling.'

The girl was surprised to hear that fearful row again, and called from her window, 'That's not my mother. She doesn't have such an awful raucous voice. Go away, you horrid creature.'

Crocodile crept unnoticed underneath the house, his long tail trailing in his wake, and he lay there muttering to himself angrily.

Presently, Leah's mother came to the shack and sang out her song loud and clear. At once Leah opened the door and let her mother in. They hugged and kissed, sat down to eat and gossip, and continued likewise until it was time for the mother to return.

But Leah held her mother back. 'O Mother, I am frightened here alone,' she cried. 'Let me come back home with you.'

'No, my daughter,' her mother said. 'I cannot take you back without your father's word. First I must go and ask him. Wait here and mind you don't open the door to anyone but me.'

Thereupon, she dashed off home to tell her husband of their daughter's fears.

'If she is scared,' Leah's father said, 'then bring her home at once. Who knows, perhaps some cunning animal wants to eat her! Hurry back for her straightaway.'

But the mother was weary from her journey and said she would go at the usual time next day. Despite her husband's protests, she insisted, 'Our daughter is quite safe. I've instructed her not to open the door to anyone but me.'

Early next morning, just after daybreak, Crocodile went back to the brawny blacksmith.

'Brother Blacksmith,' he said, 'I am exceedingly foolish. I did not do as you instructed. Since I was mighty hungry, I ate some bananas and some sweet mangoes. Pray forgive me and use your iron on my tonsils once again.'

This time the blacksmith heated the iron until it was white hot. Then he thrust it so hard down Crocodile's throat that white smoke and steam poured out and filled the forge. Crocodile leapt so high in pain that he almost hit the roof.

When the operation was complete, the blacksmith said, 'Now sing out loud, so that I can hear your voice quite clearly.'

Crocodile sang. His voice was even more shrill and sweet than before. And he was very pleased.

'Mind you eat nothing for a whole day,' the blacksmith said. 'For if you do, your voice will be worse than ever.'

Crocodile waddled away to Leah's house as fast as his stumpy legs would carry him; he was determined not to eat a thing until he got there. Just before ten o'clock, he was standing behind the little wooden shack where Leah was living. Opening his jaws as widely as he could, he sang the song:

> 'Leah, Leah, ting-a-ling-ling,
> Honey at the door, darling,
> Sugar at the door, darling,
> Leah, Leah, ting-a-ling-ling.'

His voice rang out as shrill and sweet as that of Leah's poor mother. So without a thought, the girl unlatched the door.

And before she knew it, Crocodile had run into the house and gobbled her up!

When Leah's mother reached the shack with her daughter's breakfast shortly after, she sang her song and no one answered. Once again she sang the song. And since no one answered, this time she went into the house and found, to her great horror, one shoe and three buttons. Nothing more.

As she ran out she saw the fat-bellied crocodile, snoozing contentedly underneath the shack and she realised the terrible fate her daughter had met.

When she reached home, of course she told her husband all the dreadful things that she had witnessed. Though he blamed her for not listening to him, there was nothing more to do about it.

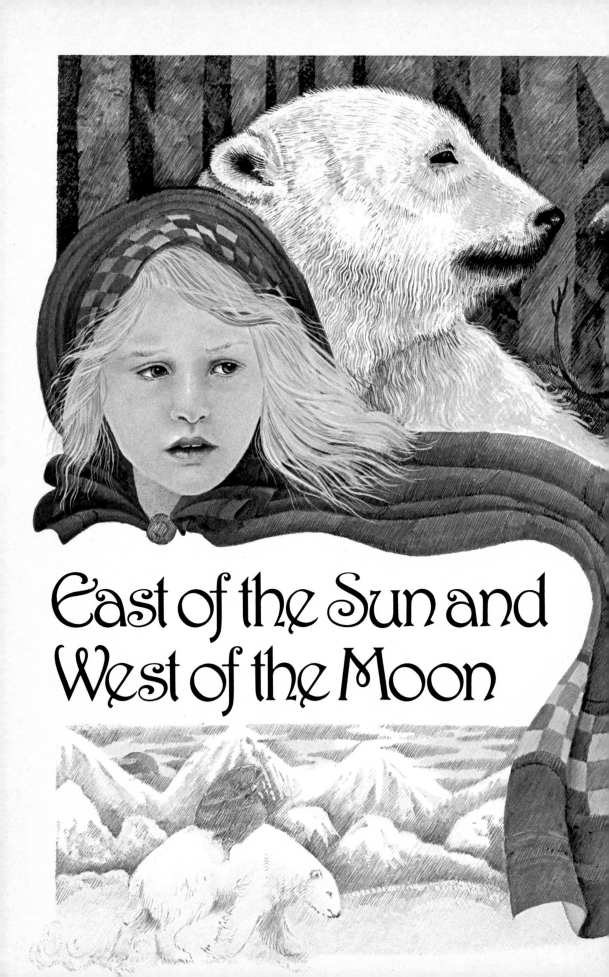

East of the Sun and West of the Moon

There once lived in Norway a farmer and his wife whose only fortune was a household of eleven sons and one daughter. The poor children had to go hungry and ragged even in the harshest snows of winter. In spite of their poverty, the boys without exception were brave and kind and the young daughter was so pretty there was none to match her throughout the Norselands.

One time, late in autumn, the entire family was sitting round the fire in the old cottage; outside the wind howled, the rain lashed the windows and it was fearful dark. Then, all of a sudden, a knock came at the cottage door.

Startled, the old farmer went to see who it could be. He opened the door and caught his breath. For there before him stood a huge white polar bear.

'Good evening to you,' said the polar bear.

'Good evening,' mumbled the man.

'I've come to seek a wife,' said the bear. 'Give me your only daughter and I'll make you as rich as you now are poor.'

The old man scratched his head. How pleasant to become rich overnight; yet he did not wish to lose his dear daughter.

'Well now,' he said, at a loss for words, 'come back in seven days and you shall have my answer.'

The polar bear shuffled off, and the old man told his family about the conversation. As soon as the beautiful young girl heard that she was being courted by a bear, she burst into bitter tears.

'Now, now, my dear,' her father tried to comfort her. 'We would not make you go against your will. Let that be an end to the matter.'

From that moment on, the poor girl knew no peace. She gazed sadly at the thin bodies of her brothers, their ragged clothes and pinched features, and her heart ached.

So when seven days had passed and the white bear returned, the girl had made up her mind.

'So be it, Father,' she said bravely. 'I'll go with the bear.'

She washed and darned her few clothes, tied her belongings in a little bundle, put on her cloak and was ready for the journey. At his command, she sat astride the bear's broad back, held on tightly to his white fur and waved farewell to all her family.

When they were already far from her home, the bear asked her whether in her heart she felt afraid.

'No, that I'm not,' she spoke up firmly.

'Then, hold on tight, for we shall move like the wind,' the bear said.

He ran along over the rocky ground as lightly and quickly as if he were flying. Finally, he halted at the foot of a tall mountain, tapped with his paw upon a rock and there before them suddenly appeared great iron gates. These gates opened by themselves, allowing the bear to pass through into a glittering underground cavern. To the girl's amazement, they went through rooms that gleamed with silver and gold until at last they came to a splendid hall. There in the centre stood a sturdy oaken table set with all manner of tasty dishes.

The bear commanded the girl to descend and be seated at the table. Then he handed her a silver bell which, he said, she was to ring whenever she wanted something. Thereupon he departed and she was left alone.

The girl drank and ate her fill, as never in her life before. She tried at least a dozen tempting dishes from among the hundred ranged before her.

After such a long journey and sumptuous meal, she was naturally very sleepy. So she rang her little bell and straightaway found herself within a bedchamber where all was ready for her. The soft bed had a swansdown mattress, silken pillows and a velvet eiderdown with golden tassles.

No sooner did her head touch the pillow, however, than she heard footsteps in the next room.

'Who can it be?' she wondered aloud. 'It is quite unlike the shuffling of the bear's great paws, yet I've seen no humans here.'

Quietly she rose, crept to the door of the next room and peeped through the keyhole. The sight within astonished her. There upon the bed sat a handsome young man! His face was very troubled and at his feet lay a white bear's skin.

In fact, though the girl was not to know it, the polar bear was really a bewitched prince who could cast off his bear skin only at night. As soon as day broke he turned back into a bear.

The days passed. Although the bear was kind and gentle to the girl, she longed for human company. A bear was a bear, after all, and not a man.

He, poor beast, knew the reason for her sorrow and tried to show himself as little as he could. But at last her tears and unhappy countenance touched his heart, and he promised to take her to see her parents and brothers.

'But you must promise me one thing,' he said. 'Should your mother wish to speak to you alone, do not consent. Should she try to learn any secrets you may have uncovered here, do not tell. I myself do not ask you what you know or might suspect. Have patience and be true, or dire misfortune will befall us both.'

She gave her word and mounted on the white bear's back and he bore her home.

She no longer recognised her former humble home upon the hillside. In its place there rose a lofty mansion with corner towers and many balconies, with pretty carvings on the windows and with tiled rooftops.

'Here is your house,' the bear said. 'Now remember your promise to me.'

'I shan't forget,' the girl exclaimed.

In the twinkling of an eye the bear was gone.

When her mother and father set eyes upon their daughter, their joy and tears could find no bounds. Her brothers almost overwhelmed her with their kisses and fond embraces. None of them could thank her enough for the happiness she'd brought. But she, poor girl, how was she faring? Did the bear treat her kindly? Was his den so terrible? They asked her many questions.

The young girl put their minds at rest. She too lived well. Even though her home was at the very heart of a mountain, it was not at all like a common bear's den; it was more like a wonderful palace. She told them all about the little silver bell, her swansdown bed and all the wonders of her new home. But of the bear himself she said not a word.

Her mother became suspicious, but no matter how much she pressed her daughter, she learned nothing more. After dinner, the mother called her daughter to her room. But, recalling her promise, the girl refused to go. All the while she found excuses: to chatter with her dear brothers, to see every wonder of the mansion, to run about the gardens.

Yet her mother would not be denied and at last found a means to lure her daughter to an empty room. When they were alone she made her daughter tell all she knew about the polar bear.

'Ah, I knew it,' said the mother. 'That bear is certainly a troll; he can turn himself into whatever form he likes. Now I'll tell you what to do. Take this wax candle and at nightfall light it and carry it into the bear's bedchamber. Cast the light upon his face, but be careful not to drop wax on him lest he wake. That would be the worse for you.'

So badly did she frighten her daughter that the poor girl was ready to do anything her mother said.

At the appointed hour of the evening, the polar bear returned for the young girl. She said goodbye to her family and set off on her return to the underground palace.

Before they had covered half the distance, the bear asked her whether she had kept her word.

Unable to tell a lie, the girl confessed to what had passed between her mother and herself.

'Oh dear,' the bear sighed. 'What's done is done. But, I beg you, do not do as your mother commands. Just be patient for a little longer and you will learn all there is to know.'

The girl had grown fond of the gentle bear and felt sorry for him. She did not really believe her mother's story that he was an evil troll. Yet when she returned to the palace and lay down to sleep in her bedchamber, all her fears came back to her.

In the depths of the night, she slipped out of bed, lit her wax candle and crept on tiptoe into the bear's bedchamber. Stealthily she went up to his bed and raised the candle above him. As the light fell upon his face, she saw clearly that he was not a troll. He was, in fact, the handsomest young man she had ever seen. Yet even in repose his face was full of sorrow.

The girl bent over him to take a better look and, in so doing, she tilted the candle and three hot drops of wax fell upon the young man's breast. He woke up with a start and stared at the girl in horror.

'What have you done!' he cried, covering his face in his hands. 'Now both of us are doomed. If only you had listened to me and waited just three more days, you

216

would have saved me. You see, an evil witch killed my father and turned me into a polar bear. All because I would not wed her ugly daughter. So now I am a bear by day, and only at night, when no one can see me, do I become a man again.

'If you had lived with me for one full year, the spell would have been broken. Now all is lost. Tomorrow I shall be far away, locked in the castle of the witch and her ugly daughter who is spiteful and cruel. I am now doomed to marry her.'

The girl wept at what she had done. 'Tell me at least the way to this castle so that I might follow you,' she cried through her tears.

'That's the trouble,' said the young man. 'There are no paths leading to that castle. It stands on an island that lies east of the sun and west of the moon. No one knows the way there.'

Next morning, when the girl awoke, both the white bear and the palace had vanished. She found herself alone, sitting in a glade in a dark forest, with just her little bundle by her side. She cried in shame until her eyes held no more tears, then, picking up her little bundle, she set off she knew not where.

For many days and nights she walked until she came at last to a lofty crag under which stood a tiny cottage. By its side on a log of wood sat on old, old woman spinning a fine silver thread on a golden spinning wheel.

The girl told the old woman her story.

'Ah, so you're the maid who did not keep her word,' the old woman said.

'Yes, it is I,' the girl confessed. 'But I love him and would do anything to rescue him.'

'I cannot tell you where the castle is that lies east of the sun and west of the moon. But I'll lend you my swift steed who will take you to the North Wind. He knows many places and, perchance, may take you there.'

Off rode the girl for many, many days until she felt the icy blast of the North Wind's breath. With a shiver she pulled her cloak more closely round her and buried her face in the horse's warm mane. At last she came to the door of the North Wind's house of ice and knocked politely. He appeared at the door, wild and raging, sending white clouds of frosty air above the girl's fair head and making her shake with cold.

When she explained her errand, the North Wind calmed down and told her, 'The castle lies a good way off, farther even than I have ever been. But if you really want to go, I'll take you on my back and try to blow us there.'

With that the North Wind puffed himself up until he was so big and fierce it pained the eyes just to behold him. Then off he rushed through the skies, on and on across the raging seas until he scarce could draw a breath, that weary was he. His broad wings began to droop and he sank lower and lower until his winged feet brushed the white wave crests. But the sight of a distant island gave him renewed force and, with one last breath, he blew the girl upon the shore just beneath the castle. She had come at last to that enchanted land east of the sun and west of the moon.

Looking down from his window, the prince was overjoyed to see her. 'Tomorrow is my wedding day,' he said. 'But I have a plan for you to save me. Listen closely: in the morning I shall say that I wish to test my bride. I shall give her my shirt with the three wax spots to wash; if she can wash it clean then I shall marry her willingly. Of course, she will fail because only a person of pure heart can remove the spots.'

Thus it was. Next day the prince told the ugly bride that he had sworn to marry only a wife who could wash his shirt clean, the shirt he wished to wear for the wedding.

'That is no great task,' she said with a noisy snort.

Yet when she began to wash and scrub as hard as she could, the wax spots grew big and black, and the shirt was even dirtier than before. And when her mother helped her with the washing, the shirt became as black as soot.

'You have failed,' the prince exclaimed. 'Since you cannot wash my shirt clean, you are unfit to be my wife. Outside the palace sits a beggar girl; I'm certain even she can do better than you.'

With that, he went to the window and called down to the girl to come into the palace. When she appeared he asked her, 'Can you wash this shirt clean?'

'I can but try,' the girl replied.

Scarcely had she dipped the shirt into the water than it became as white as driven snow.

'It is clear your heart is pure,' the prince exclaimed in triumph. 'So you shall be my wife.'

Thereupon the old witch and her ugly daughter flew into such a rage that they burst upon the spot. And all the witches living in the castle must have burst too, for no one ever saw or heard of them again.

As for the prince and his lovely bride, they walked hand in hand from the castle and were borne back by the North Wind to the girl's family in the mansion on the hillside. And there they lived for the rest of their days in peace and great happiness.

But from that day to this, nobody else has ever found the way to that enchanted castle on the island that lies east of the sun and west of the moon.

Notes for the reader

The stories told in this book are based on folk tales from all over the world. No overall theme connects them, except that of love and beauty, wit and tolerance. They are as diverse as the people that nurtured them, ranging from the ribald humour of the African tale *Kwaku Ananse and the Python,* to the hauntingly beautiful Welsh story *Dafydd and the Lady of the Lake,* from the eerie English graveyard yarn *The King of the Cats,* to the gently exotic Mongolian story *The Fern Girl.*

I have chosen only those tales which seem typical of their country of origin and its culture, and which were neither brought by conquerors nor told by the conquered. There are two exceptions: Hans Andersen's *The Little Match Girl* and Washington Irving's *Rip Van Winkle.* Both seem representative of an age and a people that are not otherwise catered for in this book.

Although I have generally tried to retain the feeling, rhythm, colour and storyline of the originals, I have not always confined myself strictly to folklore versions— embroidering here, snipping off there, tidying up and toning down, thus to create interesting, coherent tales for young people of today. Where possible I have delved into the culture and folklore history of a people, trying to recreate their manner of storytelling by translating and consulting original materials.

For the benefit of those interested in the background to the stories, I provide the following few notes and a list of books consulted.

Kwaku Ananse and the Python. In Twi, one of the chief languages of West Africa, the word for 'spider' is 'ananse', and the 'Spider Man' is the main character in many folk tales of the Ashanti people of Ghana, from whom this story is taken. These 'spider' stories crossed the ocean with African slaves, turning Ananse into Anancy in the Caribbean and Aunt Nancy in the southern states of America. In the oral tradition, many words and phrases are repeated several times to make them stronger. I have tried to reproduce this effect in the story.

Death's Godson. This macabre yet moving tale is taken from the Spanish *La muerte quiere ser madrina.* It is traditionally Spanish in its rather beautiful treatment of, and preoccupation with, death. It was translated for me by Isobel Heald, to whom I owe my thanks.

The Man Who Sold Words. This is a popular folk theme throughout the Orient. This particular version was recorded relatively recently, in 1959, from a Dungan (Hui) storyteller Chan Tian-Hai. The Dungan or Hui people live mainly in the Hansi province in northern China, not far from the Great Wall (mentioned in the tale).

The Selkie Wife. In Scotland, a bannock is a round oatmeal cake; brose is a kind of oatmeal porridge; a bairn is a child; dinna is do not; hae is have; hame is home; ken is know; meester is master; na or nae is not; peerie is tiny; wad is would; ye is you; yon is that, and a plaid is a long piece of woollen cloth worn over the shoulder.

Scarface. This beautiful legend of the Blackfeet (Siksika) Indians contains a typical Indian (and Eskimo) explanation for the origin of the sun, moon and stars. Most Indian tribes believe that there are several worlds, one above the other and that the ground of one world is the sky of the world below. Some worlds are above our earth, others below it. Each one has a hole in the top of its sky, usually at the foot of the polar star. The heroes of a number of tales fly up through the hole in their sky (or reach it by walking towards the dawn where the gradual rise of the road leads to the sky, or by walking along the path of a rainbow, or by flying up in the smoke of a funeral pyre) and people of the upper world may look down through the hole upon the world beneath them.

The Beauty of Life. This lovely tale from the green and pleasant land of Georgia in the Caucasus Mountains was first recorded in 1890 by T. Razikashvili from an itinerant storyteller, Solomon Gulishvili. I have translated it from a Russian translation of the original Georgian.

Six Blind Men and an Elephant. A fanciful elaboration of an old Indian folk tale.

Beauty and the Beast. This somewhat unusual version of Charles Perrault's famous fairy tale—surely one of the most beautiful of all tales—is taken from a story told by the 19th century Russian writer Sergei Aksakov, as recounted to him by his French nurse. It is included in his book *The Childhood Years of the Bagrov Family* under the title *Alenky Tsvetochek (Little Scarlet Flower)*. I originally translated it from the Russian when I was staying in the same district of Bashkiria as Aksakov's country estate: an inspiring setting.

Five Monstrous Creatures. An unusual version of the famous Grimm story *The Four Musicians of Bremen*, taken from the German.

Ngarri Jandu and the Nimmamoo. Adapted from an Aborigine legend collected by the intrepid Irishwoman Daisy Bates, who spent over forty years (1899–1945) living among Australian Aborigines.

Jack O'Lantern. This is just one of many stories about the tussle between a witty mortal and the Devil (or death). It is similar, for example, to the Russian *Death and the Soldier* and the Welsh *Billy Duffy and the Devil*. This version was originally taken down in Gaelic from an old Limerick farmer. I have tried to retain the flavour of

my own Irish grandfather's rich speech.

The Children of Sky and Earth. This story from Maori mythology contains a pantheon of superior gods common to Polynesia. To save confusion I have excluded many demiurges and masters of the elements from the original, and I have reversed the roles of Papa and Rangi: to Maoris, Papa is, in fact, the earth god and first woman; Rangi is the sky god and forbear of men. The version of the story given here was originally collected in 1851.

The Fern Girl. This most moving story has several versions common to Mongolian-Tartar tribes. This particular version was first recorded by a Russian political prisoner Ivan Khudyakov (1842–76) who was exiled for life for his part in the assassination of Tsar Alexander II. He was sent to the coldest inhabited place on earth, Verkhoyansk, in north-eastern Siberia, where he lived in the crowded hut of a poor Yakut. He survived just three years, until, driven mad by the conditions, he died in an Irkutsk mental asylum at the age of thirty-four. Before his death, he learned the Yakut language and gathered Yakut folk tales; his work was published posthumously in 1890. I translated this tale from the original edition while working in the folk archives of Yakutsk in Siberia.

Heesi's Millstone. This version of how the sea became salty is common to all Finnish peoples, including the Estonians and the Karelians. I have taken this story from a collection of Karelian folk tales. Karelia, formerly part of Finland, is now in the USSR.

The Devil's Gauntlet. I have here taken the liberty of putting together two of the best-known French-Canadian folk tales: *La Chasse Galerie* and *Le Loup Garou*. In translating them I have tried to retain the long, rambling, redolent sentences of the French, as they seem to keep the flavour of the lumber camps and the backwoods, and of the essentially oral tradition.

The Flying Cherry Tree. A Samurai was a member of a class of knights in feudal Japan who served their clan chiefs according to the strict bushido code of loyalty, honour and self-sacrifice. Hence the idea in the story of the Samurai's word being his bond.

The Demon of Stone Mountain. A Vietnamese tale translated from the French.

Kotura, Lord of the Winds. I collected this Samoyed or Nenets folk tale during a folk-lore expedition to north-eastern Siberia in 1977. Hunger and death from cold and starvation were constant companions of the natives of the far north. People supposed that cruel spirits were the culprits, and these had to be appeased—sometimes by human sacrifices as in this story.

Ixtla and Popocatepetl. This story is based on an old Aztec legend.

The Ugly Girl. This story is based on an old Sudanese tale. In the original the figure symbolising the girl's good nature was portrayed as a man.

The King of the Cats. This is my own version of a traditional English folk tale which I have set in the West Country—for no better reason than that I was brought up there.

Rip Van Winkle. This is a shortened version based on the famous story by the American novelist Washington Irving (1783–1859). In his *The Sketch Book of Geoffrey Crayon, Gent.*, he includes his short stories *Rip Van Winkle* and *The Legend of Sleepy Hollow.* I have tampered only slightly with the original by replacing some archaic language and, of course, shortening the story.

Anaeet. This beautiful old legend from the ancient lands of the Armenians gives some evidence of the strong matriarchal influence in days gone by (compare it with *The Beauty of Life* from neighbouring Georgia).

The Little Match Girl. This moving parable of the inhumanity of the rich to the poor is typical of much of Hans Christian Andersen's satirical work. I have translated it from the original.

Basil Fet Frumos. This ubiquitous hero of countless Romanian tales invariably enters the world in a magical way, sometimes from out of a maiden's tears or sometimes, as here, from the fragrance of the basil plant. Note the conventional opening of the tale to warn readers of the fable to come, and the ending that insists 'they live on still'.

Dafydd and the Lady of the Lake. It might help in reading this story to know that in Welsh, w is pronounced like 'oo'; y is pronounced like 'u' (as in 'but'); c is pronounced as k; ch as in the Scottish 'loch'; dd as 'th' in 'breathe'; f as v; ff as f; s as ss; ll is a spirant 'l' (rather like 'thl' or 'khl'). The accent is nearly always on the last syllable but one: thus, Dafydd is Dávith; Nelferch is Nél-verkh.

The Sweet-Voiced Crocodile. It is difficult to find a West Indian tale that does not have a direct ancestry in Africa. Here I have replaced the leopard in the original story by a crocodile, for the West Indian setting.

East of the Sun and West of the Moon. The most well-known of the Norwegian folk legends recorded in the last century by Peter Christen Asbjørnsen (1812–1885). Here shortened and translated from the original.

Acknowledgements

I would like to record my gratitude for help and advice to Vera Jacques, Director of Bradford Children's Library Services; to my colleagues Tony Hartley and Elizabeth Murtha and to Isobel Heald.

Books consulted

Tales of an Ashanti Father, Peggy Appiah, London, 1967

Cuentos Españoles, A.F.H.A. International S.A., Madrid, 1969

Dunganskie narodnye skazki i predaniya, B. Riftina (ed.), Frunze, 1975

Scottish Folk Tales, Ruth Manning-Sanders, London, 1978

Folk Tales of the World: North America, A.W. Crown, Leeds, 1964

Skazaniya i legendy, M. Chikovani (ed.), Tbilisi, 1963

Alenky tsvetochek, S. Aksakov, Moscow, 1972

Die älteste Märchensammlung der Brüder Grimm, Heinz Rölleke, Geneva, 1975

Tales told to Kabbarli. Aboriginal Legends, collected by Daisy Bates and retold by Barbara Ker Wilson, London, 1972

Irish Folk Tales, Jeremiah Curtin, Dublin, 1944

Polynesian Mythology and Ancient Traditional History of the Maori as told by their Priests and Chiefs, G. Grey, Christchurch, N.Z., 1956

Verkhoyansky sbornik, Ivan Khudyakov, Irkutsk, 1890

Karelskie skazki, U.S. Konkka (ed.), Petrozavodsk, 1977

La chasse-galerie. Légendes Canadiennes, H. Beaugrand, Montreal, 1973

Skazki dnya i nochi, A.P. Glob, Moscow, 1976

Contes de Viet-Nam, Paris, 1949

Mexican Folk Tales, Juliet Piggott, London, 1973

Egyptian and Sudanese Folk Tales, Helen Mitchnik, Oxford, 1978

More English Fairy Tales, Joseph Jacobs, London, 1894

The Sketch Book of Geoffrey Crayon, Gent., Washington Irving, New York, 1820

H.C. Andersen's liv og digtning, C. M. Woel, Copenhagen, 1949

Moldavskie skazki, A. Stolova (ed.), Kishinyov, 1965

The Welsh Story Book, W. Jenkyn Thomas, Cardiff, 1957

West Indian Folk Tales, Phillip Sherlock, London, 1974

P. Chr. Asbjørnsen, Mannen og livsverket, K. Liestøl, Oslo, 1947